SIGNPOST TO LOVE

The Earl looked down at Baptista. Her face was hidden against his shoulder.

"I am ... sorry," she said in a muffled voice. "It was ... my fault." He asked me if I ... had ever been ... kissed," Baptista said in a hesitating little voice, "and I told him ... I thought it ...would be very ... wonderful ... but I was thinking of you ... not him."

The Earl stiffened, but he did not speak and after a moment she lifted her face to look up at him.

He looked at her, thinking it would be impossible for any woman to look more lovely or so pure and untouched.

Then, as if he could not help himself, his arms tightened and slowly, as if it was a moment he would savour and remember, his lips came down on hers.

He could feel the ecstasy she was experiencing vibrate from her lips to his, and awaken in him sensations he had never known before.

It was so perfect that for a moment he was dazzled by it, as if they were both enveloped by a light that was divine.

Bantam Books by Barbara Cartland
Ask your bookseller for the titles you have missed

Barbara Cartland's Library of Love series

Books of Love and Revelation

Other books by Barbara Cartland

Signpost
to
Love

Barbara Cartland

SIGNPOST TO LOVE
A Bantam Book | December 1980

ISBN 0-553-14360-3

Published simultaneously in the United States and Canada

Bantam Books are published by Bantam Books, Inc. Its trade-
mark, consisting of the words "Bantam Books" and the por-
trayal of a bantam, is Registered in U.S. Patent and Trademark
Office and in other countries. Marca Registrada. Bantam
Books, Inc., 666 Fifth Avenue, New York, New York 10103.

PRINTED IN THE UNITED STATES OF AMERICA

0 9 8 7 6 5 4 3 2 1

Author's Note

In 1870, two years after the time of this novel, the *Duc* de Gramont began to assume an aggressive attitude towards Germany. He called the French Ambassador in Berlin to precipitate a crisis. William I of Prussia, who was taking the waters at Ems, received him with great courtesy. But the King was being pushed by Bismarck as the Emperor Louis Napoleon was being pushed by the *Duc* and the Empress.

The French Press began to stir up war-like feeling. On July 28, the Emperor joined the Rhine Army headquarters at Metz. He was in such pain from the stone in his bladder that it was agony for him to sit on his horse.

On September 2, debilitated by the stone and by prostate trouble, he surrendered with his army at Sedan. Two days later, the mob surged into the Tuileries Palace and the Prussians were marching on Paris.

Someone scribbled "Rooms to let" on the Palace walls, the Crown jewels were hidden in a Naval arsenal at Brest, and in 1887 they were auctioned: the Monarchy was finished.

Chapter One

1868

The Earl of Hawkshead was in a bad temper.

He lay back in his travelling-carriage, which had just crossed the Channel with him on his yacht, and there was a frown between his grey eyes.

He had in fact been extremely annoyed when the Prime Minister, the Right Honourable Benjamin Disraeli, had sent for him.

Usually the two men, so opposite in every possible way, got on well together, but the contrast between them was very obvious as they faced each other in the Prime Minister's room in the House of Commons.

Benjamin Disraeli, flamboyant, almost Oriental, with his jet-black hair, his large nose, and his fondness for glittering rings, looked up at the Earl towering above him with a smile on his thin lips.

The Earl, over six feet two inches tall, with broad shoulders tapering down to his narrow hips, was the acme of fashion, and yet there was something very masculine about him and also an aura of power which the Prime Minister appreciated.

He had a respect for dominating men just as he liked women who were soft, feminine, and clinging.

"I sent for you, My Lord," he said to the Earl, "as I wish you to do me a favour."

"I should be glad, Prime Minister, to do anything within my power," the Earl replied.

1

"Then I hope you will find it not too arduous a task," the Prime Minister said, "to leave for Paris immediately."

"For Paris?"

There was no doubt that the Earl was surprised.

"Suppose you sit down and let me tell you about it," the Prime Minister suggested.

The Earl obeyed him, but the expression in his eyes as he watched the man opposite was not one of pleasure.

He did not wish to leave London at the moment, not when he had several excellent horses he was planning to race and a very attractive woman engaging his attention.

"I have been hearing," the Prime Minister said, "extremely disturbing reports concerning the French attitude towards the Germans' escalation of their Armed Forces."

The Earl looked surprised.

"Surely you are not suggesting," he said after a moment, "that the French are thinking of going to war? I thought they learnt their lesson last time."

"That was what I had hoped," Mr. Disraeli replied. "At the same time, I can speak frankly and say that you and I both know that the Emperor is an unstable character and given to impulsive actions without counting their cost."

The Earl nodded his head.

Enough had been seen of Louis Napoleon, when he was in exile in England, to make it clear that he was a strange man who was not really the right type of character to lead the French.

"The Empress, as is well known," the Prime Minister went on, "is vain, frivolous, and insatiably ambitious—a dangerous combination!"

"Dangerous indeed!" the Earl agreed. "But I cannot believe that any Frenchman would be stupid enough not to realise that Germany is, and always will prove to be, a tough and almost invincible enemy."

"That is exactly what I want to investigate," the Prime Minister said, "and because I think the Emperor always looked on your father as a friend, and because you know a great number of the men now in the seats of power in Paris, I want you to discover, if you can, what is their general attitude towards Germany, and if France might intend to provoke and declare war."

"I cannot believe there is the slightest chance of that!" the Earl exclaimed. "Moreover, if it is a question of war, it is Germany that will make the first move."

"I am not certain," the Prime Minister said reflectively, "and I am disclosing State secrets, My Lord, when I tell you I have learnt confidentially that the *Duc* de Gramont, who loathes the Germans, is doing everything he can to push the Emperor into an indiscretion which might even destroy the French nation as we know it."

"He cannot be such a fool!" the Earl ejaculated.

"The *Duc* is very friendly and intimate with the Empress."

The Earl understood only too well what the Prime Minister insinuated.

The Empress Eugénie wanted victories, and she saw herself, as she always had, at the head of a great Dynasty, admired and acclaimed by all the Crowned Heads of Europe, who she always thought treated her patronisingly and looked down on her because she had not been born Royal.

The Earl gave a somewhat exasperated sigh.

"I understand what you want me to do, Prime Minister," he said, "and I will, as you ask, leave for Paris as soon as possible."

"Thank you, My Lord," Mr. Disraeli replied. "I am extremely grateful. I am not flattering you when I say there is no-one else to whom I could entrust such a delicate mission with such confidence, and I know that you, as no-one else could, will bring me back the truth."

The Earl was aware that the Prime Minister was always very flattering when he had something to gain by using the honeyed words which came so easily to his tongue.

At the same time, because he knew that in this case Mr. Disraeli spoke in all sincerity, he was gratified.

At the same time, he thought it would be extremely inconvenient to tear himself away from London.

As it was the beginning of May, the Season was in full swing, and there were Balls and parties every night given by his friends who would be dismayed at the thought that he could not be present.

The Earl had also just begun an extremely passionate liaison with Lady Marlene Stanleigh. She was the wife of a committed and ambitious politician who found his Constituency and the sound of his own voice in the House of Commons much more alluring than his wife.

Lady Marlene was acclaimed not only as the greatest beauty in the Social World but also as the gayest and most amusing.

She was witty and sophisticated, and she made any man on whom she bestowed her favours feel he was more than fortunate at being allowed to possess her.

She had for some months been acutely aware that the Earl was, to all intents and purposes, avoiding her and she had been determined to capture him.

She was, however, far too clever to show him or anyone else her intentions, and although they met surprisingly frequently—the Earl found himself continually sitting next to her at dinner or supper—he was not quite certain whether it was intentional or just chance.

He found her amusing and he liked the way she said daring, sometimes outrageous things with a *double entendre* which made him wonder if they were meant or whether she was just naïve.

It was only when finally she surrendered herself—or it was he, without being fully aware of it, who did the surrendering—that he found that she was without exception the most ardently passionate woman he had ever known.

She was clever enough not to bore him by being

over-effusive, and she still managed to be elusive when he least expected it, so, although the chase was over, he found himself still pursuing her.

She intrigued him and that for the Earl was something which had far too often been missing in his many love-affairs.

"I shall miss you madly, my handsome Irvin," she said the night before he left for Paris.

They had enjoyed a *tête-à-tête* dinner by candle-light in her heavily scented *Boudoir,* then had moved into her bedroom to lie together in the canopied bed with its silk sheets and lace-edged pillows.

"I shall miss you too, Marlene," the Earl replied, "and I promise I will not be away longer than I can help."

"That is what I want you to say," Lady Marlene answered, "and, darling, when you get back we must talk about our future together."

The words were spoken very quietly, but the Earl heard them, and although she was very soft and compliant in his arms, somewhere in his mind a little red flag of danger began to flutter.

He kissed her forehead, then rose from the bed.

"No! No!" she protested. "You cannot leave me so soon!"

"I have quite a number of things to do before the morning," the Earl answered, "and I would also like a few hours' sleep."

"I want you—close to me."

"You must wait until I return."

The Earl began to dress himself quickly and expertly.

It always infuriated his valet that he was capable of looking after himself if it was necessary and even the intricacies of his evening-clothes presented no particular difficulty.

"Where will you be staying in Paris?" Lady Marlene asked petulantly.

"With the *Vicomte* de Dijon. He is an old friend and I am always welcome in his house in the Champs Élysées."

"I will write to you there," Lady Marlene said,

"and, dearest, wonderful Irvin, if I do not hear from you I swear I shall be distraught."

She paused, then added:

"It will be quite safe if you send your letter in an envelope addressed to my lady's-maid as you have done before."

Again the red flag was waving in the Earl's mind.

Letters were always dangerous, and the short notes he had sent her in the past, addressed in a surreptitious manner to her maid, had contained nothing more incriminating than the time of a *rendezvous* or an invitation to dinner.

He walked to the bedside to look down at Marlene.

With her long hair tumbling over her shoulders and her skin translucent like a pearl against the silk sheets, she was very alluring and very provocative as she held out her arms to him.

"I will dream of you until you return," she said.

The Earl took her hands and kissed them one after the other and her fingers tightened on his.

"Somehow, some way, we must be together for —eternity!" she whispered.

"Good-bye, Marlene."

He walked across the room to the door. Then when he would have turned the key and opened it, he heard a faint sound outside.

Had he not been standing at the door it would have escaped his notice, but as he listened he knew that somebody was coming slowly and quietly up the stairs.

There was a creak as if from a loose floor-board, then an unmistakable footfall.

With the swiftness of a man used to danger, the Earl moved to the window.

"What is it? What is the matter?" Lady Marlene asked.

The Earl did not reply, he merely pulled aside the curtains and stepped out through the window onto the small wrought-iron balcony.

All the houses in the street had them and he

was aware that the wall of Lady Marlene's room adjoined that of the house next door.

There was an almost identical balcony about four feet away and the Earl regarded it contemplatively.

Then he was aware, although he had closed the curtains behind him, that Lady Marlene had risen from the bed on which he had left her lying naked and was moving across the room to the door.

He heard the key turn in the lock, and without hesitating any longer he climbed swiftly onto the side of the balcony and jumped.

He landed neatly in the very centre of the balcony next door and saw there was a window open wide enough for him to squeeze through.

He found himself in a bedroom identical in size to Lady Marlene's, and he was aware that there was somebody in the bed.

As he parted the curtains to enter the room, he must have been silhouetted against the starlit sky outside, for there was a little scream, then a woman's voice asked:

"Who—are you? What do you—want?"

The voice was not that of someone very young but perhaps middle-aged or old.

"I beg your pardon," the Earl replied. "I am afraid I have come to the wrong room!"

He walked towards the door as he spoke, opened it, and proceeded without hurry down the stairs.

It took him only a few seconds to unbolt the front door and let himself out into the street.

Then he walked away in the direction of Berkeley Square and his own house.

*　　*　　*

Now, driving towards Paris, he was aware that by sheer luck he had escaped being involved in a situation which might have had disastrous consequences.

It had never struck him for one moment that Lady Marlene wanted more from him than a short

and passionate liaison in which they both accepted
the rules of the game and would, when the fires of
desire died down, part without any animosity on either
side.

Now he vaguely remembered hearing that Stanleigh was not only indifferent to his wife but bored
with her succession of lovers.

He had not listened when he had heard this, for
the simple reason that he did not believe it.

He was well aware that a beautiful wife whose
father was the distinguished Duke of Dorset was a
distinct acquisition when it came to rising in the
political field.

What was more, although they were continually
hard up, it was Lady Marlene who provided what
money they had to live on, and in such circumstances
there was no chance that Stanleigh would cease to
be a complaisant husband.

Now he remembered how, on two occasions last
month, he had seen Leonard Stanleigh in the House
of Commons with Miss Sarah Vanderhof.

On the last occasion they had been sitting on the
terrace talking so earnestly to each other that he had
passed them without their even noticing him.

Sarah Vanderhof was an American heiress who
had been much acclaimed in the newspapers because
of her father's enormous donations to Charities.

Pretty and glittering with a wealth of jewels
which would not have been considered good taste
on an English girl, Miss Vanderhof already occupied
a unique position in the Social World.

Now the Earl began to understand what he had
been extremely obtuse in not realising before.

Leonard Stanleigh wanted money, and if he
married a great heiress like Sarah Vanderhof he
could do all the things that were out of reach of his
pocket now.

The only stumbling-block was that he was already married, and divorce, which had to go through
Parliament, would mean unpleasant publicity and
would also be extremely expensive.

Everything would be far easier if his present wife, Lady Marlene, agreed to co-operate.

As the plot unveiled itself before the Earl's eyes he felt like a man who had escaped destruction by a hair's-breadth and had been rescued when he was on the very point of drowning.

"How could I have known—how could I have guessed for one moment that Marlene wanted marriage?" he asked himself.

As he looked back he thought there were in fact many pointers which might have warned him that she would find marriage with him desirable.

She had asked him to show her the unique collection of jewels that were worn by every Countess of Hawkshead.

At the time he had been amused that the huge tiaras of diamonds, sapphires, and rubies so obviously delighted her. Now he knew that the expression in her eyes had not only been one of admiration but one of greed and desire.

It had not been surprising that she found his houses and his vast Estates the sort of background she wanted for her own beauty.

Hawk in Sussex was one of the most magnificent early Georgian buildings in the whole country. Hawkshead House in Berkeley Square had been in the family since it had been built 130 years ago, and his paintings and treasures were unrivalled in any London house of the same size.

"How could I ever begin to guess that she intended to be my wife?" the Earl asked himself.

He had in fact been quite shaken at having such a narrow escape, knowing that however desirable he found her, Lady Marlene was the last sort of woman he wanted as his wife and the mother of his children.

He was not quite certain what he did desire in that capacity, but Heaven knows his relatives had talked about it often enough and beseeched him almost on their knees to marry and, by having a son, to ensure the continuity of the family.

He found himself thinking of his grandmother,

who was the last person who had talked to him on the subject and had made a great deal of sense, although he had not thought so at the time.

"You are getting on in age, Irvin," she had said sharply, in a clear voice that sounded younger than her years.

"I am aware of that, Grandmama," the Earl had replied with a smile, "but I daresay I shall last a few years more."

"It is time you were married, and you know it," the Dowager said. "You cannot go on playing about with doxies until you are on two sticks, and I want to see your son before I die."

"That gives me another twenty years."

"You know perfectly well that is most improbable," his grandmother replied, "and you will be thirty-four next birthday. Your father married when he was ten years younger than you are now."

"So you have often told me," the Earl said. "Grandpapa, if I remember right, was nearer my age."

"He was thirty-two," the Dowager answered, "and he told me he had been looking for me all his life."

"There you are!" the Earl exclaimed. "I am following in Grandpapa's footsteps and waiting for someone as lovely and intelligent as you were at eighteen. But they are not to be found these days."

"You are flattering me," the Dowager said. "At the same time, you know as well as I do, Irvin, that you need a wife, and as it happens I have the exact girl in mind for you."

The Earl grinned.

"I guessed what this lecture was leading up to, Grandmama, and quite frankly I am not interested."

"You have not seen her yet, and when you do, you will know she is the right sort of person who would embellish our family-tree and look right at the head of your table."

"If that were as near as I would have to get to her, I would accept your suggestion with pleasure," the Earl answered. "Unfortunately, Grandmama, I know that any woman whom I married would bore me to distraction within a month of the Marriage Ceremony, if I had to see her for breakfast, luncheon, tea, and dinner."

"That is nonsense!" the Dowager retorted brusquely. "You have a busy life and there would be no need for you to spend more than a few hours with her every day, and even then you would not have to be together."

"Is that really your idea of marriage, Grandmama?" the Earl asked in surprise.

As he saw the twinkle in his grandmother's eyes he knew she was laughing at him.

"I refuse!" he said firmly. "I categorically refuse here and now to be pressured into marriage with any tiresome, unfledged girl, or someone who will 'look right at the head of my table' but will be a crashing bore in bed!"

It was the sort of thing he would not have said to anyone but his grandmother, who had a Georgian sense of humour and was far more outspoken than any Lady of Queen Victoria's Court would have dared to be.

The Dowager Countess laughed.

"Very well, Irvin," she said. "I give you six months in which to find yourself a wife who lives up to your own expectations. After that, I shall produce my protégée and use every means in my power to make you take her up the aisle."

The Earl smiled drily. Up until now he had managed to avoid being inveigled into matrimony by having nothing to do with young girls.

In fact, he very seldom met any.

The house-parties he enjoyed, and in fact the only invitations he accepted, were those given by the sophisticated social set that circled round the Prince and Princess of Wales at Marlborough House.

The parties they gave and those at which His Royal Highness was a Guest of Honour did not include young girls, but only the type of alluring and beautiful married women whom the Prince and gentlemen like him found amusing.

"As you have threatened me and made me extremely apprehensive as to my future," the Earl said to his grandmother, "I will now say good-bye."

"Do not forget, Irvin, I give you six months," his grandmother said, "and actually I think if you put your mind to it, we could start planning the wedding before the summer is over."

"Now you really have terrified me!" the Earl said as he kissed her hand.

She had laughed at him, and he knew as her eyes lingered on his face that she loved him more than she had ever cared for her own children, whom she had always found somewhat of a nuisance.

He had driven away from her house determined to pay no attention either to her threats or to her pleadings.

Now, after the shock of learning what Lady Marlene was intending, he told himself that his grandmother was right and he should be married so as to protect himself from the traps of fortune-seekers who wanted him not as a man but for his position and his wealth.

He was really astounded that Lady Marlene should contemplate the social ostracism which would result from a divorce.

He would be forgiven because no stigma was ever attached to a man who disobeyed the social code, but for a woman it was different.

Then he knew that while Lady Marlene would not be accepted at Court even as the daughter of the Duke of Dorset, after a little time had elapsed she would, as the Countess of Hawkshead, creep back into the good graces of the Prince of Wales.

"She had it all worked out," the Earl said to himself, "and after a few years in which she would be content to be spending my money in Paris, Rome, or Venice, she would be welcomed back by her friends with open arms."

He considered how in many ways she could buy her way back into their good graces, with huge house-parties at Hawk and lavish entertaining in Berkeley Square.

It was lucky that the jump between the two buildings, which would certainly have been beyond the capabilities of a less athletic man, had presented no difficulty for him.

He wondered if Stanleigh, after he had been let into the bedroom by his wife, had gone onto the balcony and, finding no sign of him, looked down to the basement below, wondering if he would see his body spread-eagled on the railings.

At the same time, the whole episode had left him in a bad temper.

If there was one thing the Earl disliked, it was being, in his own words, "had for a mug."

He also prided himself that he was far too experienced not to be able to judge a man or a woman's character shrewdly.

Where Lady Marlene was concerned he had failed, and he had lain awake last night asking himself how he had not been clever enough to sense what she was up to long before he had nearly been trapped like any greenhorn up from the country.

"Dammit, I am not going to think of her again!" he told himself, but the rough weather only added to his bad humour.

He was a good sailor and was not in the least sea-sick, but he worried about his horses, which were frightened at sea, and he had also found the best Hotel in Calais, at which he stayed the night, inferior to the Hotels he occasionally patronised in his own country.

The food, however, was good and after a large breakfast the Earl proceeded to ride one of his own horses while the outrider perched on the box of the carriage.

He always found it convenient to travel not only with his own carriage drawn by four horses but with two outriders so that he could take exercise whenever it suited him.

The morning was fresh, but when the sun began to grow hot, the Earl with a gesture of his hand drew the carriage to a stop and continued the journey in comfort.

Wearing powdered wigs, white breeches, and close-fitting liveries, the outriders added a touch of colour and indeed elegance to the black and yellow travelling-chariot with its magnificent team of four jet-black stallions.

The Earl had every intention of riding again later in the day, but now there came a sprinkle of rain.

As he put his feet up on the seat opposite him, thoughts of Marlene came back to irritate him, so that he sat with what his old Nurse would have called "a little black devil on his shoulder."

Deep in his thoughts, he did not realise that the carriage had come to a sudden standstill, until the footman on the box jumped down and opened the door.

"What is the matter?" the Earl asked. "Why have we stopped?"

"There's an accident ahead, M'Lord."

"What sort of accident?"

"I thinks one of them French carriers they calls *diligences* has run into a post-chaise, M'Lord."

The footman glanced over his shoulder before he added:

"Looks a reg'lar mess, M'Lord, horses an' bodies everywhere."

"Well, see if you can give them any help," the Earl replied, "and let us proceed as quickly as possible."

"Yes, M'Lord," the footman answered doubtfully, and shut the door.

The Earl told himself he had no wish to be involved personally.

It was quite usual for there to be accidents on the roads, which were often too narrow for the amount of traffic they carried, and the mails, the post-chaises, and even carriers like the *diligences* travelled far too fast.

In England the stage-coaches would round a corner at speed and crash into a farm vehicle drawn by one slow horse, or in France by two lazy white bullocks. In consequence it was no surprise that animals and people were often severely injured.

The Earl prided himself that in all his years of driving—and like everyone else he enjoyed moving at speed—he had never had an accident.

That was due, he had often thought, not to luck but to judgement—something which drivers of public vehicles seldom had.

What he hoped was that this accident would not prevent them from moving on as quickly as possible, because he wanted his horses to have a good rest tonight before they set off again tomorrow for Paris.

If he had to go to Paris when he would rather be in London, then the sooner he got there and carried out the Prime Minister's instructions, the better.

He knew quite well it was not something one could do in twenty-four hours or indeed in a week. His investigations would take time, unless he was particularly fortunate.

Even then, whatever he was told by one person would have to be checked with information from another.

He sighed at the thought of how many people he would have to call on and how he would undoubtedly have to spend long hours of boredom at the Tuileries Palace with the Emperor.

There was only one cheerful prospect ahead, which was that Paris was notorious all over Europe for the beauty and the wild and insatiable extravagances of its women.

They were certainly not the sort of "ladies" his grandmother had in view as the future Countess of Hawkshead, but their expertise in "love," although that was not really the right word for it, would certainly enable him to pass his time agreeably when he was not on duty.

He would doubtless find it an expensive diversion, but to him that was of little consequence.

He was just wondering which of the famous Courtesans he would call on first.

He had already met all those who were notorious and he knew not only that they would be amusing but that he would meet and greet many friends in their company, especially in the house of the Queen of them all, La Paiva.

He also suspected that she would know more than anyone else about Germany's intentions towards France.

"I shall call on her first," the Earl decided.

At that moment the door of his carriage opened.

"We can move on now, M'Lord," his footman informed him. "It be a terrible mix-up but there be nothin' more we can do. And there's a man helping who seems t' be a Doctor."

"Then let us proceed," the Earl said.

The footman was just about to obey his orders when the door on the other side of the carriage opened and to the Earl's surprise a woman stepped in.

As he stared at her, she sat down on the edge of the seat opposite him and said in a small, frightened voice:

"Please . . . please . . . will you take me with you . . . wherever you are . . . going? I have to . . . get away."

She spoke in English and as the Earl looked at her he thought she was very young and very lovely.

She had a small flower-like face in which her two blue eyes seemed unnaturally large.

He realised that there was an expression of shock in them, doubtless from the accident, and he saw that her bonnet had fallen from her fair hair and was suspended down her back on ribbons which tied in a bow at her throat.

There was a tear in her gown, and her ungloved hands twisted nervously, almost as if they beseeched him to listen to what she asked.

"I perceive you have been involved in this accident," the Earl said, "but surely you are not travelling alone?"

"No . . . but the . . . people with me are . . . injured and that is . . . why I have the . . . chance to get . . . away."

The Earl realised that the footman was listening.

He gave a signal to the man to shut the door, which he did, but then he stood outside so that they could see him silhouetted through the window, which had been closed against the rain.

"Now tell me what all this is about," the Earl said.

"What I am asking you to·... do is to ... take me away as ... quickly as possible," the girl answered. "It does not matter where ... just ... anywhere so that I can ... escape."

"But why? And from whom?"

"Must I tell you ... that?"

"I am afraid so, if I am to assist you."

"I will tell you everything, I promise, only must we stay here? I think one man who was with me and who calls himself a Priest is badly injured, but my father may regain ... consciousness. Then he will ... ask for me."

"Your father?" the Earl questioned. "You are trying to escape from him?"

"Yes. He is taking me as a prisoner to some terrible place which he says is a Convent, but I think it is something quite ... different. Oh, please ... please ... help me! If not, I must start ... walking or running across the fields, and I do not ... think I will get very ... far."

There was a note of terror in her voice, to which the Earl instinctively responded, but as he looked at her he saw that she was so young and obviously so inexperienced that he could not possibly become involved with her and her attempt to escape from her parent.

"I am sorry ... " he began, but she said quickly:

"I must make you ... understand what I am ... asking. My father, I think, is mad, and because my mother ran away and left him, he is ... determined that I shall expiate her ... sins for the ... rest of my life."

"What do you mean by that?" the Earl asked.

"Because in appearance I am like her, my father ... intends that I shall be ... shut up in this Convent which I think is really a place of ... penitence. It is run by a Sect who punish themselves for their . . . sins by . . . flogging and other methods of . . . physical pain."

"What you are saying is unbelievable!" the Earl exclaimed. "It cannot be true!"

"I swear to you that what I am . . . telling you is the . . . truth! I am afraid—desperately afraid, and because I am rich, once they get me there they will . . . never let me . . . go! Oh, please . . . please save me!"

There was no doubt, the Earl thought, that she believed every word she was saying, but he found it incredible.

Because he was playing for time to think over what she had told him, he asked:

"What is your name?"

"It is Baptista Dunsford," she answered, "and my father is Lord Dunsford."

"Lord Dunsford!" the Earl exclaimed. "The 'Preaching Peer'?"

"Yes . . . that is right," she replied, "and you cannot know what it is like to live with him. He not only preaches hell and damnation, he . . . practises it at home. Oh, take me away! I cannot be beaten by him again or put in that . . . horrible place to which he is . . . taking me."

It was a cry for help which the Earl felt he could not ignore.

"Very well," he said after a moment, "I will take you to the nearest town, where I am staying the night. After that you must look after yourself."

"Yes . . . of course . . . and thank you . . . thank you! If I can get away now, I can find my . . . own way to . . . Paris."

The Earl bent forward to signal the footman.

As he opened the door the Earl asked:

"What about your luggage?"

"Do not worry about that," Baptista answered, "just drive away before Papa . . . realises I have . . . gone."

She spoke in a very low voice so that the footman would not hear, and the Earl replied:

"We will drive on immediately, James."

"Very good, M'Lord."

The horses were moving before he had sprung up onto the box, and Baptista gave a little cry that the Earl knew was one of relief.

Then she moved with a swiftness he did not expect across the carriage and onto the seat on which he was sitting, to cower in a corner with her hands up over her face.

He realised that she was hiding herself as they passed the scene of the accident.

From his side of the carriage he looked out the window to see the usual confusion of frightened horses, crying women, and luggage strewn over the road.

Quite a number of people were lying on the grass verge, either with injured limbs that needed attention or flat out as if they were unconscious.

There was a post-chaise in which he imagined Baptista had been travelling, but as they flashed past it was impossible to identify Lord Dunsford, whom he knew by sight.

He had in fact heard the "Preaching Peer," as he was called, declaiming in the House of Lords, but he had always determinedly left the Chamber as soon as he began.

His Lordship's theme was always the same: the wickedness that he averred was rife all over the country owing to the lack of law and order, and the stringent punishments that should be administered to the sinners in this world, which would be doubled and trebled in the next.

"Is there no way of curbing that damned fool?" a fellow Peer had asked on one occasion.

"Not unless we have him committed to an Asylum," someone had answered. "It would be the right place for him."

The Earl had merely thought Lord Dunsford a bore and he never allowed himself to be bored.

Now, looking at his daughter, he felt sorry for her even if the fantastic tale she had told him was really untrue.

They were past the accident now and the Earl sat back in his own corner of the carriage, contemplating his guest as she took her hands down from her face.

She was, he decided, very young indeed, little more than a child, and it seemed impossible that she was not using an over-active imagination in thinking that her father intended to put her in a Convent.

"I have done as you wished," the Earl said now, "and let me add that it is against my better judgement."

It struck him that this was very much the truth.

Nothing could be more reprehensible than carrying away a young girl from her father's protection, especially when she was in a foreign country.

Then astutely the Earl told himself that if there were any enquiries, he would say he had been asked to give the victim of a road accident a lift as far as the next town, and as he was alone in an empty coach, he could hardly refuse such a request.

Aloud he said:

"Now suppose you tell me the truth of why you are running away from your father."

"I have tried to run away three times already," Baptista replied, "but each time he has caught me, and the last time he beat me so violently that I could barely walk for a week."

"You expect me to believe that?"

She looked at him and for the first time she smiled, and he saw she had two dimples as she asked:

"Would you . . . like to see my back?"

"I will accept your injuries without visual proof!"

"Very well. As I have already said, I think Papa is a little . . . mad. He was always . . . strange in many ways, but when Mama left him he became very much worse."

"When did your mother leave?"

"Nearly three years ago, and since then I have felt he was watching me and hating me because I grew more and more like her. Then a month ago he met this 'Priest.'"

"You call him a Priest. Is he a Roman Catholic?"

Baptista shook her head.

"I do not think so. He calls himself a Priest but his religion is very strange and rather horrifying."

"You say your father met him—where? And how did he meet you?"

"Papa had been away in London ... I think to speak in the House of Lords ... and when he came home, he brought this Priest with him. He calls himself Father Unctious, and because he wore a cassock I thought he must be a Catholic."

She sighed before she went on:

"I was wrong, and he and Papa kept saying how people should be punished for their sins and that wickedness could only be expunged by driving the devil ... out of them."

Baptista gave a little shudder and went on:

"At first I did not listen. I was used to Papa going on and on about sinners burning in hell-fire and the terrible punishments that women who had left their husbands would receive."

She gave a little sigh.

"Of course he was talking about Mama, although he did not mention her by name. Then he would say: 'I must save you! I must save you from the bad blood that runs in your veins, from the inclinations that will rise up within you so that you too will become a disciple of the Devil!' "

"It must have been very frightening," the Earl remarked.

"I had almost got used to it, in a way, except when he beat me," Baptista said honestly, "until the Priest came. Then I realised he was encouraging Papa to become more and more ... fanatical on the subject."

She was silent for a moment before she said:

"When I came into the room they always stopped talking, and I knew they had been discussing me. Father Unctious used to look at me in a manner which made me think he was imagining how he could torture me."

She made a little movement with her hands

which told the Earl without words that she was finding it difficult to express what she felt. Then she went on:

"I began to grow frightened ... very ... very frightened. I do not know why, but I knew ... something was going to happen which ... would concern ... me ... so I ran away."

"Where did you run to?"

"I did not get very far the first time. I slipped out of the house after I had supposedly gone to bed, and I found Papa and the Priest waiting for me. I thought afterwards that one of the maids must have told him I was collecting a few things to carry with me in a parcel."

"What happened?"

"Papa dragged me back and beat me, and all the time he was doing it I was quite certain the Priest was outside the door listening to my screams, because he enjoyed the sound of them."

Baptista gave a little sob and the Earl said:

"Where were you going?"

"I was trying to get to London, to my mother's sister. I was not quite certain where she lived or even if she would be pleased to see me, but I thought she might be able to tell me where I could find ... Mama."

"You know where your mother is?"

"She went to Paris, and I know the name of the ... person she was ... with."

This obviously came reluctantly to her lips, and for a moment the Earl did not press her further. He merely asked:

"So you tried to escape again?"

"Yes, twice more, and the last time I got nearly to London in the stage-coach, but when we reached the very last stop before Islington, Papa was there waiting for me and he was very, very angry. He took me home and beat me until I fainted, then he told me what he had ... decided to ... do with ... me."

There was no mistaking the terror in Baptista's voice now as she went on:

"I was to spend the ... rest of my life in a House

of Penitence, and my money . . . I have a lot left to me by my grandmother . . . was to be made . . . over to the . . . Order. The Priest had said that he was one of the Founders . . . after that I should never be allowed . . . in Papa's words . . . 'to contaminate the world again.'"

"Can that really be the truth?" the Earl asked in astonishment. "How could your father be allowed to do such a thing?"

"I am only just eighteen," Baptista answered, "and as my Guardian he can do anything he likes with me. That is the Law!"

The Earl was well aware that this was true, and he said:

"Surely there is somebody in your family to whom you can appeal for help?"

"There is . . . nobody on Papa's side," Baptista replied, "and naturally I have not been allowed to see any of Mama's relations since she left us."

"How could she leave you with a man like that?" the Earl asked sharply.

"Papa used to beat her too," Baptista said. "He said she was too beautiful and was a . . . temptation from which he must . . . purge himself."

"He is mad!" the Earl said violently.

"Yes, I know," Baptista agreed. "But what can I do about it?"

The Earl was aware that it would be impossible for her to bring her own father to justice or, for that matter, to escape from him in the first place.

"What happened in the accident?" he asked.

"We were driving along in the post-chaise which we engaged at Calais. Papa and I were sitting on the back seat and the Priest on the opposite one."

She shivered and said in a low voice:

"He was watching me in that horrid manner that made me want to scream. Then suddenly as we went round a corner we heard the man driving us shout: 'Look out!' There was a dreadful crash and there seemed to be a lot of people all screaming at once, before I was thrown out of the carriage and onto the side of the road."

She paused and then went on:

"There was thick grass, and though I was stunned for a moment I was not hurt. Then as I sat up I saw that we had hit a *diligence* and there were people thrown into the road and the poor horses were down on their knees. There also seemed to be a lot of blood everywhere."

Baptista drew in her breath as if at the horror of it before she continued:

"Then I saw that Papa had half-fallen out of the carriage and was lying still, with his eyes closed. The Priest, who was lying on the road, had a gaping wound in his forehead which was bleeding and it looked to me as if he was dead."

"What did you do?" the Earl asked.

"I could only think that this was my chance to get away. I looked to one side of the road and saw there were fields stretching into the distance. There were no hedges where I could hide, and I thought that when Papa regained consciousness he would see me and I would be brought back and . . . beaten."

Baptista paused, and the Earl had a fleeting glimpse of her dimples as she said:

"Then a little way up the road I saw your wonderful horses and your smart carriage!"

She paused before she added:

"I felt it was Elijah's chariot from Heaven, come to deliver me!"

The way she spoke made the Earl laugh.

Chapter Two

They drove for a little while in silence. Then the Earl asked:

"You expect to find your mother in Paris?"

There was a distinct hesitation before Baptista replied:

"I ... hope she will be there. I knew when she ran away that was where she was going."

"Why?"

Again there was a silence before Baptista replied:

"Mama went ... away with ... the *Comte* de Saucorne."

The Earl raised his eye-brows. He thought he knew the name but he could not put a face to it.

"And you have heard no more since she left?" he asked after a moment.

Baptista shook her head before she said:

"Because it made it worse for Papa that Mama should prefer a Frenchman to him, he chose France as the place where I should do penance for her 'crime.'"

The Earl thought that in a mad sort of way he could understand the twisted manner in which Lord Dunsford's brain worked, but he found it difficult to credit all that Baptista had told him.

She was so small and exquisite, so flower-like in her appearance, that it was hard to believe that any man who was supposed to be a gentleman would beat anything so fragile or indeed want his own child to be punished for another person's sins.

And yet, from all he had heard of the "Preaching Peer," his whole attitude towards wickedness was concerned not with saving people but with punishing them.

Sitting comfortably at his ease against the heavily padded cushions of the carriage, the Earl could see Baptista's profile and thought that her beauty in one way or another would always cause trouble.

Although he knew little about very young women, he was aware that she was not only exceptionally lovely but also had an elegance and a grace of movement which he would have expected only in a far older woman.

He also suspected that despite her child-like appearance she was intelligent.

This he found to be true when two hours later they stopped for luncheon.

As they drew into a Posting-Inn which the Earl knew in the past was, if not good, at least one of the best on the main route to Paris, Baptista looked apprehensive.

As if he could read her thoughts, the Earl said:

"You are quite safe. Even if your father is now in hot pursuit of you, it is doubtful if any post-chaise —and I imagine he has had to procure himself another—could catch up my team of four, and we shall not stay here longer than necessary."

"You are . . . so kind," Baptista murmured, "but I was really wondering if you would want me to . . . leave you now and find my . . . own way from here."

"Suppose we talk about that over luncheon?" the Earl suggested. "I think it constitutes a problem to which we should give our full attention."

He saw her eyes light up and knew it was because he was concerning himself with her rather than with being rid of her at the first opportunity, as he had suggested.

When she had gone upstairs to tidy herself and he had been shown into a small private Dining-Room, he told himself that although he had no wish to be brutal, he must rid himself of Baptista as soon as possible.

There was no reason why Lord Dunsford should connect him with her disappearance from the scene of the accident.

At the same time, if he made enquiries it was likely that someone might tell him that there had been an impressive-looking travelling-carriage there, and although the odds were against it, somebody might have seen Baptista stepping into it.

After the narrow escape he had just had in London he had no wish to find himself caught in another trap, and he therefore decided firmly that when they reached the town to which he had sent a Courier ahead to make arrangements for the night, he would say good-bye to Baptista.

It passed through his mind that perhaps, having run away with the *Comte* de Saucorne but being unable to marry him, Lady Dunsford by this time might be in very different circumstances from what her daughter expected.

Then once again he thought it was not his business and if Baptista did not like her mother's way of life, she could always return to her father.

At the same time, he was in fact shocked by what she had told him about the place to which she was being sent.

The Earl had heard that there were many fanatical Sects in France at this time, ranging from Anarchists to the Followers of the Rosy Cross, and he presumed a House of Penitence would come within the category of religious extravagances which were bound up with Louis Napoleon's reign.

It sounded to him rather sinister and he thought it was more than likely that the so-called Priest had been excited at the idea of Baptista's fortune being used to further his work.

"Dammit all, the whole thing is unpleasant and unhealthy!" the Earl said to himself.

But there was nothing he could do about it and the sooner he stopped thinking about it the better.

The door of the room opened and Baptista came in.

She had tidied herself and her hair gleamed gold in the sunlight coming through the window, and her eyes were very blue.

She looked so young, so spring-like, and so lovely that the Earl had a sudden vision of her being humiliated and beaten, and he felt himself shudder.

"I hurried," Baptista said with a little lilt in her voice, "and I am sure luncheon will be delicious. French food is so good!"

"You prefer it to English?" the Earl asked.

"The food we have at home is very austere since Mama left," Baptista replied, "and when Papa has a

Fast-Day, which is once a week, we have only dry bread to eat and water to drink."

"I wonder your father considers that sufficient sustenance to enable him to continue his preaching," the Earl said sarcastically.

"Papa likes doing penance, although what for, I cannot imagine," Baptista answered. "He never commits any sins, although he constantly refers to himself as 'a miserable sinner.'"

She smiled and her dimples were very prominent as she said:

"I find it difficult to be miserable unless somebody is punishing me, and I never have a chance to commit any sins, unless you count running away as one."

"I would have thought it very wise of you to run away if you had somewhere to go," the Earl remarked.

He saw by the expression on Baptista's face that she knew he was not speaking lightly, and she said quickly:

"I have always been determined . . . that I would somehow join Mama. I am sure she would . . . miss me, and I have . . . missed her."

There was a little note of doubt in Baptista's voice which told the Earl that she might be frightened that her mother would not want her.

"I am sure she will be delighted to see you," he said reassuringly. "Now let me give you a glass of Madeira. I think you have earned it after such a dramatic morning."

"It was certainly that," Baptista agreed. "At the same time, think how lucky I was to find you!"

She smiled at him before she added:

"You might have been a disagreeable old man who would refuse to give me a lift, or a thief who might have abducted me for my money."

The Earl thought she was much more likely to have encountered a man only too ready to carry her off for her beauty, but aloud he said:

"Have you any money with you?"

He asked the question casually, thinking from

the way she had talked that Baptista was likely to have provided herself with funds just in case she had a chance to escape from her father.

Therefore he was not prepared for the blush that suffused her face and the way she turned her head aside in what was an obvious movement of embarrassment.

"I was going to ... talk to you about ... that," she said after a distinct pause.

The Earl was about to speak, when the Landlord came bustling into the room followed by two mob-capped maids with a number of dishes which they set down on a table which was laid near the window and on a side-table near it.

There was also a bottle of champagne in an ice-bucket, which the Earl had ordered, and the Proprietor said:

"If you will be seated, *Monsieur et Madame,* the meal may commence."

"*Merci,*" the Earl replied, and did as he requested.

Baptista came slowly to the table and he knew from the way she did not look at him that she was still embarrassed.

They were served the first course, champagne was poured into their glasses, and after he had taken a few mouthfuls and found, as Baptista had anticipated, that the food was excellent, the Earl said:

"I feel it somewhat surprising that although we have now been in each other's company for most of the morning, you have not enquired as to my identity. It appears to me to be a strange lack of curiosity."

"It is not that," Baptista replied. "I am, as a matter of fact, very curious as to who you are, but I felt that as you had no wish to be ... involved with me, perhaps you would prefer to remain incognito so that I could quite truthfully say, if questioned, that I had no ... idea who you ... were."

The Earl was surprised.

"Do you really think I would be ashamed of offering you a helping hand?" he enquired.

Baptista looked at him seriously.

"You have been very kind, so very kind," she said, "but I am well aware that if Papa knew that you had helped me to escape, he would be extremely angry not only with me but with you, and he might make . . . trouble for you when you . . . return to London."

The Earl did not speak and she went on:

"I can see you are somebody of great importance, and it will always be tantalising to know that while your chariot appeared to have come from Heaven, I shall not be able to pray for you by name."

The Earl laughed.

"Is that what you intend to do?"

"Of course. I shall always say a very special prayer for you that you will find what you want in life, which I expect is happiness."

"Most men need something more tangible than that," the Earl said teasingly.

"A lovely lady?" Baptista questioned. "I am sure you will find one in Paris."

"What do you know about Paris?"

"Not very much," she admitted, "because Papa always considered it a cess-pool of wickedness not only because Mama went there but because he disapproves of both the Emperor and the Empress."

"Why should he disapprove?" the Earl asked in surprise.

"I am not quite certain," Baptista answered, "but one of my Governesses told me that Papa had forbidden her to teach me any history appertaining to the Kings who were immoral in their behaviour, like Charles II and of course Louis XIV and XV."

"So there is a gap in your historical education?"

"Not . . . exactly."

She looked a little mischievous as she explained:

"Of course being told that made me curious, so I searched through Papa's Library when he was not there, to find quite a lot about the lovely ladies at the Court of Charles II and many references to Madame de Pompadour and the other famous Courtesans."

"I am beginning to understand why your father

thought that a Convent was the right place for you!"

The Earl spoke severely but his eyes were twinkling.

"Now you are being very unkind," Baptista protested, "and I have already told you I was being punished not for my own sins but for Mama's."

"That, I agree, is grossly unfair," the Earl replied, "but I can understand your father not wishing you to go to Paris, unless of course you were very properly and respectably looked after."

As he spoke he knew that he was being tactless, because one could hardly describe Lady Dunsford as being respectable, but he thought Baptista was not likely to realise that he had made a "gaffe" and went on:

"It is the gayest and most extravagant city in the whole of Europe, with a sophistication which is certainly not the proper background for a young girl."

There was silence. Then Baptista said:

"There is nowhere else I can go . . . and when I find Mama I know she will . . . look after me."

"I am sure she will."

"Tell me about Paris," Baptista pleaded, "as you see it, the buildings and of course the music and literature."

She gave a little sigh.

"My Governess used to hint at all the new ideas and the interesting books that were being produced in Paris, but I was not allowed to read them."

The Earl told her of the splendour of the Opera House and the delightful and extremely intelligent Plays that were being produced in the other Theatres in Paris.

Because she was obviously entranced by everything he said, he found himself growing quite eloquent on the subjects of Offenbach's music and the artists who were making the Academie and the Salon the Art Centres of the World.

Only when luncheon was finished and he and Baptista were sipping their coffee did he return to the question he had originally asked her.

"I spoke to you just now about money," he said,

"and I would like to know how much you have with you."

"I shall be ... all right."

"That is not the answer to my question."

Baptista clasped her hands together.

"Please ... because you have helped me I do not ... wish to be an encumbrance or to make you feel you are responsible for me in any way."

"I am responsible for you whether I like it or not," the Earl said. "At the moment you are my guest, and I can hardly be so inhospitable as to turn you into the street without the means to carry you to your destination."

"I have told you that if Papa discovers that you have helped me he might make terrible trouble for you. He can be very vindictive if people oppose him in any way."

The Earl saw the little shudder Baptista gave and knew she was thinking of the way she had suffered physically when her father was angry.

"I assure you," the Earl said firmly, "I am not in the least afraid of your father or of anything he can do to me."

This was not exactly true, but he felt it was something he had to say to boost his own self-respect.

"That is why," he went on, "I feel I must inform you that I am in fact the Earl of Hawkshead."

As he spoke he wondered if it would mean anything to Baptista, and he was surprised when she gave a little cry of recognition at the name.

"Then you own Rollo and Apollo, who won the two big races last year!"

"That is true," the Earl admitted. "Rollo won the Thousand Guineas and Apollo the Gold Cup at Ascot. But I am surprised that you should be aware of it."

"I love horses," Baptista said, "and although Papa would have been very shocked if he had discovered it, I always read the racing reports in *The Times*."

The Earl laughed.

"You are certainly full of surprises, especially as you are Lord Dunsford's daughter!"

"Oh, I wish we had talked about horses while we were having luncheon!" Baptista exclaimed.

Because her tone was so fervent, the Earl replied almost without thinking:

"It is a subject which perhaps we will find absorbing at dinner."

"I may dine with you?"

He knew by the way she spoke that she had anticipated he might wish to be rid of her before then.

"I shall be very honoured if you would do so," the Earl said firmly.

He wondered whether he was being fool-hardy to the point where he was definitely inviting trouble.

He rose from the table, saying:

"Because it would certainly be sensible for you to be as far ahead of your father as possible, I suggest we waste no more time but continue on our way."

They travelled quite a number of miles before it was dusk and they came to the town in which they were to stay the night.

For the larger part of the journey they did not converse.

Firstly because after luncheon the Earl left Baptista alone in the carriage while he rode, and secondly when he returned to sit beside her, she thought he might be somewhat tired and was deliberately quiet.

At the same time, although he was not aware of it, she had been saying a little prayer of thankfulness that she had been fortunate enough to find him and that he was carrying her farther and farther away from her father.

It was difficult to explain to anyone how terrifying her life had become in the last two years when she had grown increasingly to resemble her mother and was in fact no longer a child but grown up.

Her father's hatred of her had seemed to increase day by day, and when he was not actually beating her he would continually slap her or hit her besides berating her for sins she had not committed.

She knew it was only because he was identifying her with her mother.

At the same time, it was hard to live with, and at times she wished that she could die rather than go on enduring a hatred which she knew was not normal and came from an unbalanced mind.

Her Governesses had loved her, and through reading Baptista had managed to escape into a world of her own and at times be quite oblivious to her father's thinking out excuses to persecute her.

The best way she could escape from the menace of him was by riding, and fortunately, for some reason which she could never ascertain, Lord Dunsford did not forbid her the enjoyment of riding.

Everything else either was taken away or there was a long list of things she might or might not do.

Her bedroom and Sitting-Room were stripped of all the china ornaments, the paintings, and even the cushions, because he considered them frivolous and attractive.

Her clothes were plain, austere, and inclined to be ugly.

However, the difficulty, Lord Dunsford found, was that everything once Baptista was wearing it assumed a beauty and elegance that was part of herself.

First he had tried to dress her in black, a suitable colour, he informed her, for those who must expurgate their sins.

But black merely accentuated the clear whiteness of her skin, the gold of her hair, and the blue of her eyes, and other dark colours had the same effect.

She was, of course, forbidden any of the frills, bows, and laces which were very much a part of the fashion, but again the plain bodices seemed to accentuate the soft curves of her breasts and draw the eye to her small waist.

Her travelling-gown, which was a dull, dark blue, had, the Earl noticed, made her seem very slim, and its very severity made her appear almost Grecian rather than drab and dowdy as her father had intended.

As he rode alone over the fields, keeping the coach travelling on the main highway towards Paris in sight, the Earl found himself wondering what Baptista would look like if she were dressed in the elaborate bustled gowns that Mr. Worth had made the rage in Paris.

Then he remembered that she had not yet answered his question as to how much money she had with her, and he thought that when they reached the place where they were to stay the night and she had not even a nightgown, there would be various necessities she would wish to purchase through the chambermaids.

"She must have brought some money," he told himself.

Yet because it had made her look embarrassed and at the same time very attractive he began to think that was unlikely.

The sun was sinking and the horses were growing tired when they saw the spires and roofs of a town ahead, and the Earl said to Baptista when he returned to the coach:

"When we arrive I will provide you with a room for the night."

"I think I must ... tell you," Baptista said in a low voice, "that I ... cannot afford to ... pay for it."

"That is what I suspected," he replied. "And now perhaps you will answer my question as to how much money you have with you."

"I am afraid ... none!"

"None!" the Earl exclaimed. "Then how on earth did you think you could reach Paris without any?"

"I did collect a little money in one way or another, when I ran away the last time and almost reached London," Baptista explained. "But Papa took it from me, and because he was determined that I should not escape again, he made one of the servants search my room two or three times a week. He only gave me money to put in the plate at Church when we were actually in the pew, and he watched to see that I did not steal it."

"So how are you going to manage?" the Earl asked.

"I just hoped that a . . . miracle would happen," Baptista answered simply, "and when the accident occurred, all I could think of was getting away . . . and as I have already said, there you were . . . waiting . . . like an answer from Heaven."

"God is said to help those who help themselves," the Earl remarked, "but I am just wondering what will happen to you if I drive on tomorrow without you, as I intended to do when you first asked me for a ride in my coach."

"I should quite . . . understand if you did that," Baptista said, "and I would not . . . blame you in the . . . slightest."

She spoke quietly. At the same time, there was a look of pleading in her eyes which the Earl could not ignore.

"You really must be sensible enough," he said sharply, "to realise the dangers if you travel alone to Paris without having any money."

"No-one could . . . steal anything from me," Baptista protested.

The way she spoke and the questioning look in her eyes told the Earl that she really did not understand that most men who saw her would not want money but something very different.

Because he had a feeling she was going to question him, he said quickly:

"I will take you to Paris and hand you over to your mother. Another time be more sensible and realise that one cannot eat or travel unless one can pay for it."

"I . . . did know that," Baptista said meekly. "It was just that . . . there was no possible way I could get hold of any money, with Papa watching me . . . and although I prayed and prayed to be delivered, I was terribly afraid that my prayers would not be answered."

"Well, they have been!" the Earl said uncompromisingly, "and you now have to show a little common sense."

She looked at him enquiringly.

"For one thing," he went on, "we could hardly arrive in Paris without making some explanation as to why you are with me, and the interpretation most people would put on your presence would not be good for your reputation."

Baptista looked puzzled for a moment, then she said:

"You mean people might think . . . because I was unchaperoned . . . that I was a . . . Courtesan like Madame de Pompadour?"

"That is one way of putting it," the Earl fenced.

Baptista gave a little cry.

"But that is fascinating! I would love to be a woman whom men thought so alluring and beautiful that they built a Theatre for her, as Louis XV did, and painters, sculptors, and china-makers all over France brought her their work to gain her approval."

"I am not actually a King," the Earl said mildly.

"At the same time, you are very important," Baptista insisted, "and as you own such magnificent horses I am sure that the French consider you a King of the Racing World . . . and if I could be your special Courtesan . . . then I could ride your horses."

"Are you suggesting, in a somewhat obscure manner," the Earl asked, "that you should ride with me tomorrow?"

"Oh . . . could I . . . please . . . could I do that?" Baptista cried. "It was an agony watching you ride over the fields while I had to sit in the carriage. I can ride well, I promise you, and as I am so light . . . I would not tire a horse as much as you do."

"You make it sound very plausible," the Earl said. "What about your clothes?"

"I do not suppose the horses will mind what I am wearing," Baptista replied, "and you need not look at me."

"I have the uncomfortable feeling," the Earl said,

"that you are one of those women who get their own way by means that are not obvious to a mere man."

Baptista did not reply. She merely looked at him with pleading eyes, and after a moment he said:

"All right. You can ride tomorrow, and if you arrive in Paris looking a mess, you must not blame me."

"I look terrible anyway," Baptista said. "Papa would never allow me to have pretty gowns and he burnt everything that belonged to Mama."

"Burnt?" the Earl questioned.

"Yes, he made a bonfire in the garden on the lawn and everything was taken out of her bedroom and thrown onto it. Her bonnets, her furs, her shoes, even her sunshades. I cried . . . but Papa said prayers all the time they were burning."

The Earl thought that if he read such a story in a book he would not believe it.

As he heard more about Lord Dunsford, he was quite certain that he was insane. At the same time, a madman could be extremely dangerous and he had no wish to draw Lord Dunsford's attention to himself.

"What I was going to suggest, Baptista," he said, "when you diverted my train of thought, was that while we are travelling together you should become my niece."

Baptista considered this, putting her head a little to one side.

"Are you old enough to be my uncle?"

"I most certainly am!" the Earl said positively. "You are only a child and I am in fact practically middle-aged."

Baptista laughed.

"No-one would believe that, and you are very impressive."

"Is that how I appear to you?"

"I expect to everybody. You walk as if you have bought the earth on which your feet rest, and when you look down your nose at anyone, I feel quite certain they flatten themselves on the ground."

"I have a feeling you are laughing at me," the Earl said.

Baptista's dimples made little dents in her cheeks.

"I would be much too frightened to do that," she answered, "and really I am admiring you. I think you are magnificent and just what an Earl should look like. It is only a pity you are not a Duke."

"I am sorry you are disappointed."

"Not disappointed," Baptista said quickly. "How could I be? And I expect the French will feel overwhelmed the moment they see you."

"Let us get back to my idea of your being my niece," the Earl suggested. "I will instruct the servants that your name is Miss Baptista Hawk, which is, of course, my family name."

"It suits you," Baptista said. "Although I think you should have been an eagle, which is the King of birds!"

"I have the feeling," the Earl said, "that as my niece you should be more respectful and certainly not so personal."

"But I am saying nice things!"

"Too nice, and too intimate," the Earl answered. "You should remember that if I were really your uncle you would be in awe of me."

"But I am," Baptista said. "But perhaps it would be more fun if I were your Courtesan."

"Fun or not, that is something you cannot be and must not pretend to be," the Earl said sharply. "Get it into your head that you are my niece until the time when we find your mother and I can hand you over to her."

"You make me sound exactly like a parcel you wish to be rid of," Baptista said a little wistfully.

Then, as the Earl did not say anything, she asked:

"Am I really such a . . . bother and a . . . bore?"

There was something pathetic in the way she asked the question, and because the Earl felt sorry for her he replied:

"I admit you are rather a worry, but you are certainly not a bore, Baptista. And I am looking forward to the conversation we can have at dinner about my horses."

For a moment he was dazzled by the smile she gave him.

Then they were driving through the narrow cobbled streets of an ancient town to the Hotel de Poste, where the Courier whom the Earl had sent ahead from Calais was waiting on the door-step to greet them.

The Earl explained, in a voice loud enough to be heard by anyone who was interested, that his niece, Miss Baptista Hawk, had been involved in an accident on the road outside Calais and he had brought her with him, although unfortunately her luggage had been left behind.

He repeated more or less the same story in French when explaining why he needed an extra room on the same floor where his Suite was situated.

This was arranged, and as they went downstairs to the Sitting-Room the Earl said to the Courier:

"Miss Hawk will of course require certain things for the night, and as her gown has been torn in the accident, perhaps you could find a shop open, even at this late hour."

"There should be no difficulty about that, M'Lord."

"Then see what you can do," the Earl said.

He saw the excitement in Baptista's face and he added:

"I suggest, my dear niece, you tell Mr. Barnard exactly what you require, and he will have it sent to your bedroom while you rest before dinner. As I also wish to rest, we will dine a little later than usual, and that will give him time, I hope, to purchase you a new gown."

Baptista looked at him a little enquiringly, and he said to the Courier:

"When you have made the purchases, Barnard, bring all the accounts to me."

"Yes, of course, M'Lord."

The Earl went to his own bed-chamber, where Stevens, his valet, who had driven ahead with Mr. Barnard, was waiting for him, having ready a bath, as was expected.

As this always entailed a great commotion in a French Hotel, the Earl made a point of congratulating the man.

"I hope you had a good journey, M'Lord," Stevens said as he helped the Earl out of his coat.

"There was a very nasty accident outside Calais," the Earl replied, "and it was extremely fortunate that I came along just by chance at the right moment to rescue my niece."

He was well aware that Stevens, who had been with him for fifteen years, would know that Baptista was not his niece, nor did he have one of that age, but Stevens was far too acute and shrewd not to understand exactly what his Master wanted of him.

"That was certainly a fortunate coincidence, M'Lord," he said. "And will Miss Baptista be coming with us as far as Paris?"

"Yes, Stevens, and when we reach there she will have to stay with us until I can make other arrangements for her."

He knew as he spoke that Stevens would realise that the servants of the *Vicomte* de Dijon would also have to believe that Baptista was his niece.

That should not be difficult because, although the *Vicomte* was a great friend and had often stayed with the Earl in London and at Hawk, he had never met either of the Earl's married sisters, who were older than he was and who lived for the most part in the country.

Once again the Earl told himself that he was being extremely foolhardy and if such a subterfuge were discovered it would undoubtedly cause a great deal of gossip if not scandal.

At the same time, he could not think what else he could do.

Baptista's looks and youth and innocence made it completely impossible for him to let her travel alone or to arrive in Paris without some sort of Chaperone.

If Paris was known as the City of Gaiety, it was also the city of a great many other things as well.

The vice that was not far below the surface was

not only to be found amongst the *Grandes Cocottes,* the mistresses of the Emperor and gentlemen like him in search of amusement, but was actually part of the whole structure of French life.

This made it, as the Earl was well aware, quite impossible for anyone like Baptista to walk about the streets alone, and certainly she could not stay at any Hotel or Boarding House, even if they would accept a woman who was unaccompanied.

'I got myself into this and I have to get myself out!' the Earl thought.

Yet he knew that if he abandoned Baptista to her fate, it would be an act as reprehensible and even as criminal as anything her father contemplated for her.

* * *

When the Earl, extremely impressive in his evening-clothes, went into his Sitting-Room two hours later he was not surprised to find it empty.

He had never known a pretty woman, he thought, who had not kept him waiting.

But there was a bottle of excellent champagne on ice, and as he poured himself a glass he thought that if he was honest, Baptista had managed to make his journey up to now more amusing than he had expected it to be.

Because he was a very active man both mentally and physically, the Earl found long journeys extremely tiresome unless he was driving or riding.

He also, like most Englishmen, disliked dining alone, especially in an Hotel.

He knew that even the food and wine, which he had expected to be good, would not have compensated for the boredom of sitting at a solitary table at a Restaurant or, as he had intended, alone in his Sitting-Room.

But because Baptista was with him and he found her, he told himself, an interesting study, he was looking forward to dinner and, as she had requested, telling her about his horses.

The door on the other side of the Sitting-Room opened and a voice asked:

"Are you there?"

"I am," the Earl replied.

"Then hold your breath, because I am going to appear!"

The Earl smiled and waited and a moment later Baptista walked into the room.

She stood still dramatically, her arms open wide, compelling his attention.

Then she turned round and he saw that the gown she was wearing had a full bustle at the back, and she glanced over her shoulder to see if he was appreciating it.

Then she turned round again.

"Look at me!" she cried. "Do you see how different I am from the way I was before? Oh, please ... please tell me you think I am ... pretty!"

That was certainly an understatement, the Earl thought.

He knew that the white gown Barnard had chosen, while certainly not in the same class as the gowns that could be purchased in Paris, had a French *chic* which would not have been procurable in any provincial town in England.

It was the height of fashion and swept to the back where it was caught by a large bow of stiff silk before it billowed out in a small train.

The bodice was very tight and off the shoulders with a bertha of gathered lace.

It made Baptista look, the Earl thought, rather like a small angel, except that the excitement in her blue eyes and the smile on her lips made her delectably human.

"I have never had a gown like this ... before," she said in a breathless little voice. "How can I ... thank you?"

"I have been thinking," the Earl replied, "that I should thank you for making my journey far less tedious than it would otherwise have been and for entertaining me in a very delightful manner."

She gave a little cry of joy and ran forward.

"Do you really mean that?"

"I have just told you so," the Earl replied. "Now let me give you a glass of champagne."

"If only I could give you something," Baptista said, "I should not feel so ... guilty at taking so ... much."

She paused to say:

"I am afraid I am ... costing you a lot of ... money."

"Most women do that in one way or another," the Earl replied.

"I am sure if I were a Courtesan it would be much, much more."

"That is the sort of remark I should not expect my niece to make to me!" the Earl said severely.

Baptista paused for a moment to see if he was really annoyed. Then when she saw that he was not, she said, looking at him from under her eye-lashes:

"I think it very unlikely that any uncle would look like you."

"On the contrary," the Earl objected, "I have several nieces and nephews."

"And the girls are as pretty as I?"

"They may be in the future," he replied. "My oldest niece is, to the best of my knowledge, about eight years old."

"Then I am unique," Baptista said complacently, "and that is what I want to be. I was thinking when I was trying on these beautiful gowns that ..."

She paused, then said:

"You did mean me to have two—one for tomorrow?"

"Is that what Barnard bought?"

Baptista nodded.

"Oh, please, it does seem a little greedy ... but my other gown was torn."

"I am delighted to give you two gowns," the Earl said, "and anything else that is necessary at this moment."

"Oh, thank you ... thank you!" Baptista cried.

"How can you be so kind and so wonderful? I promise that one day I will repay you."

"How do you expect to do that?"

"Perhaps when I am with Mama I shall find a rich husband, or, as I was just going to tell you, I was thinking it might be rather fun when I am in Paris to become a Courtesan."

The Earl did not say anything and she went on:

"I was trying to remember what I had read about Madame de Pompadour in a book I found once, and it said how hard she tried to please the King, but was very worried because she did not like him making love to her."

There was a little pause, then Baptista said:

"I expect that meant she did not like him kissing her. But I do not understand why she did not like it when she had agreed to be his Courtesan."

The Earl drank a little of his champagne, then he said:

"There is no reason for you to worry your head about Madame de Pompadour or any other Courtesan, and it is certainly something you will never be yourself."

"Why not? If the King can have a Courtesan it cannot be wrong."

"Louis XV has been dead a very long time," the Earl said, "and things have changed today."

He hoped he might be forgiven for lying, because the Emperor of France flaunted his mistresses openly for all to see.

Only in England had Queen Victoria's reign produced an outward show of morality, which while publicly acclaimed was certainly not followed by the Prince of Wales.

"That is a pity," Baptista said, "because it must have been very exciting in the past to have the position that Madame de Pompadour occupied."

"There were certain hazards attached to it," the Earl remarked drily. "Perhaps your history-books omitted to inform you that Madame du Barry was guillotined."

"I remember that," Baptista said. "But why? What did she do?"

"She associated with Louis XVI."

"Oh . . . I see. Then perhaps after all it would be safer if I remained your niece."

"That is what you will appear to be," the Earl said firmly, "and as I have already told you, any niece I possess would not talk about Courtesans. Keep to conventional subjects of which anybody would approve."

"I will be very careful to do that," Baptista answered, "but only when anyone else is there. When I am with you I can talk frankly about all the things that really interest me."

"And that should be horses," the Earl said, and he nearly added: "We will keep off the subject of love in whatever form it appears."

They talked about his horses all through the dinner, which was brought to their Sitting-Room.

Baptista was a little disappointed that they were not to dine downstairs in the Restaurant.

"I have never dined in a Restaurant," she said, "and perhaps there are people there who would like to see my gown."

"I doubt it," the Earl answered, "and anyway I intend to dine upstairs. But if you wish to eat downstairs alone, I shall accept your decision."

He had spoken crushingly but Baptista laughed.

"Now you are being ridiculous!" he said. "And I am quite certain there would be no tall, handsome, exciting noblemen like yourself, but only small, rather insignificant Frenchmen."

"They would not be pleased to hear you speak like that," the Earl said, "and may I point out, Baptista, that people who are related as a general rule do not admire each other or pay compliments."

"You are making it very difficult for me," Baptista protested. "I want to tell you what I think and what I feel, and if that is wrong you will have to forgive me because I have never dined alone with a gentleman before."

She smiled and added:

"All I can think about at the moment is that because by taking me to Paris you have saved me from Papa, you are the most wonderful man in the whole world!"

The Earl gave up the hopeless task of trying to convince Baptista that she was not to address him in such a manner.

Instead he talked of art, about which he found surprisingly she knew quite a lot, and once again of Paris, in which she was absorbedly interested.

Because it was in his mind, he found himself describing to her some of the political figures he hoped to see, and when they had talked until the dinner was finished and the servants had left the room, she said:

"I may be wrong, but I have the feeling that you are not going to Paris just to enjoy yourself."

The Earl was startled.

He realised that he had been talking to Baptista not in the way he would have talked to Marlene or any other woman of his own set with whom he might have been dining, but almost as if she were a man, especially while he was describing to her the statesmen he would meet in the French Capital.

"Why should you think that?" he asked.

"Because you are so clever," Baptista answered, and at the same time so attractive, I cannot believe that you have to go to Paris just to amuse yourself, especially when you have two horses running at Epsom next week."

It was a shrewd assumption, the Earl thought, but he was not going to admit it.

"I shall be back in time for Royal Ascot," he said, hoping it was true.

"I would love to see you win the Gold Cup," Baptista said wistfully.

"I might not be so fortunate this year, although I have two horses that I am considering running in that race."

"But you will try to win."

"Of course every owner does that, but in these classic races where all the horses are outstanding there is always an element of luck, perhaps in the number one draws, if the going suits a particular horse, or if one's jockey is as clever as one hopes he will be."

"Everything in life depends a little bit on luck," Baptista said. "I remember Mama saying once: 'One is very fortunate if one is born beautiful, clever, and into the right position in life, but to be happy one also needs love and that is often unpredictable.'"

"I suppose your mother was thinking she was unlucky to have married your father," the Earl said cynically.

"Of course she was," Baptista agreed. "She was only seventeen when she married him, and because her parents were not well off they were delighted she should make such a good match. Then Papa began to grow very strange, and he believed, because she was so beautiful, that Mama was tempting him into sin. I told you the rest of the story. Mama's luck must have run out."

"I am afraid it had," the Earl agreed.

"I have been lucky. Very, very lucky, because I have met you."

She sighed, then she said:

"I know that when we reach Paris and find Mama I shall perhaps never see you again, but I shall always remember tonight when we dined together and all the things you have said to me."

There was a little sob in her voice that the Earl did not miss.

He looked at her with a smile on his lips and found his eyes held by hers.

He was used to seeing a look of admiration on a woman's face, but with Baptista it was different.

He could not explain to himself why it was. He only knew that once again he had an impression of danger.

It made him rise to his feet.

"If we have to leave early in the morning, Baptista," he said, "I think you should go to bed."

There was a little pause before Baptista said in a low voice:

"Yes, of course . . . if you want me to."

"I have told Mr. Barnard to try to procure a riding-habit for you before we leave. He has been with me for a long time and it is seldom he does not find what I want."

"Thank you . . . that is very kind of you."

She spoke in a low voice which was very different from her exuberance earlier in the evening.

The Earl made certain he did not meet her eyes again. Instead he put out his hand.

"Goodnight, Baptista, sleep well, and we will breakfast in here at eight o'clock."

"Good-night, My Lord."

Baptista put her hand in his. As she did so, she curtseyed, and he felt her fingers quiver in his as if he held a butterfly.

Then without looking back she went into her bedroom.

The Earl stood for a long time staring at the closed door.

Chapter Three

For the second time, driving beside the Earl, Baptista thought how lucky she was.

She had been awakened at seven o'clock that morning and the maid had brought her a riding-habit that Mr. Barnard had procured in some mysterious way from, she was sure, the best dressmaker in the town.

It was certainly very attractive, of a thin blue material that seemed to echo the blue of her eyes.

"I'm afraid it may be rather thin, Miss Baptista," he said anxiously, when she thanked him after she was dressed, "but they only have summer-clothes in stock now."

"I do not need anything thicker when I am riding," Baptista assured him.

She loved the amusing French hat which went with it and which was different from the more severe riding-hats worn in England.

She thought the Earl smiled at her appreciatively, and as soon as they were clear of the town they both mounted horses which had been ridden by the outriders.

Despite the long day yesterday, Baptista's horse was skittish and full of spirit, and the Earl noted that she handled him in an expert manner until after an exhilarating gallop he quieted down.

They rode for about two hours, then because he enjoyed both driving and riding the Earl took the reins of the travelling-chariot.

He and Baptista sat on the box-seat while the servants sat inside, and Baptista smiled as she said:

"If we drove up to a smart Hotel I am sure the porters would open the door of the carriage, where they assume the Gentry would be sitting, while you and I would be ignored."

"I feel that however obtuse the porters might be, they could not help thinking you were a strange sort of footman to grace any Englishman's carriage!"

Baptista laughed.

"Perhaps I will set a new fashion. If I do, would you engage me?"

"Certainly not!" the Earl said firmly. "I dislike women who wish to do jobs which are the perquisite of men."

"That is what I thought you would say," Baptista replied, "and I suppose you think a woman's work is in the home and nowhere else."

"That is certainly my opinion," the Earl agreed.

"What about actresses?"

"That is something quite different," the Earl said sternly, "and if you are going to tell me you are thinking of going on the stage, you can forget such ideas."

"As a matter of fact, now that you have suggested anything so exciting, I shall certainly consider it," Baptista said mischievously.

"In which case I shall immediately notify your father as to what you are doing," the Earl threatened.

"You could not be so treacherous, so under-handed, or indeed so cruel," Baptista protested.

Then she looked at him and added:

"I know you are only teasing me, but it frightens me even to think of Papa. Supposing he has caught up with us by now and will appear at any moment to take me away from you?"

She looked over her shoulder apprehensively as she spoke, and the Earl remarked drily:

"Unless your father has managed to find a carriage and horses to exceed the speed of mine and has travelled all through the night, I am convinced we have put a great many miles between him and us."

He heard Baptista give a little sigh of relief and knew that even if she had exaggerated her father's treatment of her, he still had the power to terrify her in a way which the Earl knew no father should have been allowed to do.

They had a quick but appetising luncheon in a small town, then set off on what the Earl knew was quite a long stage to where they would stay that night.

He wished to ride, but when he suggested that Baptista had taken enough exercise, she answered:

"I am not in the least tired, and I want to ride your magnificent horses. I may never have the opportunity again."

The Earl did not dispute this but lifted her onto the saddle, thinking she was very light, although she certainly had the strength to control a spirited horse.

He had always thought that a woman could look her most attractive on horse-back, but he had often found that the women he fancied lost a great deal of their allure when they were indifferent riders.

Looking at Baptista's slender figure in her well-cut, extremely *chic* French riding-habit, he thought as he had last night that if she were dressed by one of the great dressmakers either in Paris or London, she would cause a sensation in the Social World.

Then he told himself that this was something she would be unable to do because she would be hiding from her father. For at least the next three years she would have to live secretly and obscurely if there were any English people about.

He found himself wondering what her mother's position was in French Society.

As the wife of another man she could hardly expect the more respectable ladies in Paris to accept her while she was living with the *Comte* de Saucorne.

It would therefore mean that unless they were to be content just with each other's company, Lady Dunsford would know only the less respectable families or perhaps merely the *demi-monde*.

He found himself frowning at the thought that in that case Baptista would make the acquaintance of a number of very undesirable men who would expect her morals to be as questionable as those of her mother.

For the first time he began to consider whether in rescuing her from her tyrannical father and taking her to Paris he was perhaps doing her a disservice.

He was well aware that Frenchmen would find her alluring and extremely attractive.

Her fair hair, blue eyes, and pink-and-white skin were a Frenchman's idea of an English beauty.

While as her father's daughter they would treat her with respect and perhaps even consider her eligible to marry one of the sons of a noble house, in the company of her mother the proposals they would make to her would involve something very different from marriage.

The Earl was aware by now how innocent and intrinsically pure Baptista was.

Despite the fact that she had read a lot and was extremely intelligent, she was absolutely ignorant of the world and the men who lived in it.

She had indeed come up against what the Earl knew was something unnatural and repulsive in her father's obsession for punishment. But, although he recognised that it had a perverted connection with physical enjoyment, that aspect of it had never occurred to Baptista.

Even what the ordinary man desired of an attractive girl was something of which she had no knowledge, and he wondered how long she would be able to remain in such a state of innocence once she reached Paris.

"Perhaps I should turn round," he told himself, "and take her back to England and find out if there are any Dunsford relatives who would take her under their protection."

Even as he thought of it he knew that Lord Dunsford was her natural Guardian and would still have the power legally to force her to obey him and, if he wished it, to incarcerate her in a House of Penitence.

The more he thought about Baptista and his responsibility towards her, the Earl found himself "between the devil and the deep blue sea."

Whatever he did it seemed to him he would be hurting Baptista, and perhaps the lesser of two evils was to take her to her mother.

"I may find my fears on that score are quite groundless," the Earl tried to console himself.

At the same time, when Baptista looked at him with her eyes shining in her small, flower-like face, he was apprehensive about her future—a matter which had never concerned him before with the women he knew.

They had ridden for nearly two hours when quite suddenly it began to rain, and the Earl, looking at the darkness of the sky ahead, was sure they were in for a thunder-storm.

They were passing through a flat part of the country, and while there were few woods, there were, as was inevitable in France, tall high trees lining each side of the narrow roadway.

One of the hazards of a thunder-storm was that during it a tree might be struck and fall either to block the thoroughfare or, more dangerous, to land on any animal or vehicle that happened to be passing.

When the Earl and Baptista had given up their

horses to the outriders and were once again seated inside the travelling-carriage, the Earl looked out the window and knew they were driving straight into the storm.

There was nothing they could do about it but to drive on, although the Earl hoped there might be a town ahead where they could shelter until the worst of it was over.

However, he was aware that this was a thinly populated area on their route to Paris and therefore he could only hope that the storm would abate and be less violent than appeared likely.

His hopes, however, were not realised. The rain not only poured down, but the flashes of lightning and the rumbles of thunder frightened the horses.

The coachman was having difficulty in controlling them, and the footman, who was also a groom, mounted the off-side leader, as was usual in such emergencies.

To enable him to do so, the carriage stopped and the Earl said:

"I will take over the driving."

He did not wait for Baptista to reply, but got out into the pouring rain and climbed up onto the box.

They moved on and half-an-hour later Baptista was aware that they were turning into the courtyard of a small Inn.

She could see that they appeared to be on the outskirts of a hamlet, and the door of the carriage was opened by a rather rough-looking man in dirty clothing.

She saw that it was not the type of Inn which the Earl would ordinarily have patronised, but it would obviously be foolhardy to travel farther.

She walked inside to find that it was a low-ceilinged, poorly furnished place, but not as dirty as she had first anticipated, judging by the man who had opened the carriage door.

An elderly man who was obviously the Proprietor came forward to welcome her, and when she explained that they had stopped owing to the storm, he was very effusive in his offer of hospitality.

"I am sure the first thing *Monsieur* and his servants will require," she said in her good French, "is for their clothes to be dried."

That, the Inn-Keeper assured her, presented no difficulties.

There was a large fire in the kitchen and when the horses were stabled everyone would be looked after and well fed.

The Earl came in as he was speaking, and as soon as she saw him Baptista knew she was right in thinking that his clothes needed drying.

He had fortunately put on his overcoat before he left the carriage for the coachman's box, but even so it was obvious that it was soaked and even his hair was plastered down on the sides of his face.

He laughed at her expression as she saw him, and said that the coachman and outriders were in a far worse state than he was.

The Proprietor of the Inn lit the fire in the large open grate and the Earl divested himself of not only his overcoat but his smart grey whipcord riding-jacket.

Baptista found herself thinking how attractive he looked in his white muslin shirt, which fortunately had escaped a soaking, his buckskin breeches, and his highly polished riding-boots.

The Earl ordered a bottle of wine and when it came he insisted that Baptista have a glass with him.

"I do not like drinking alone," he said, "and I have a feeling that while the wine may be drinkable, the food will not be of the quality we have enjoyed so far."

"Will we have to stay the night?"

"I hope not," the Earl replied, "but so far the storm does not appear to be abating, and it can be difficult and even dangerous to drive on the wet roads unless one can see clearly where one is going."

As he spoke, a crash of thunder overhead told them that the storm was still with them and Baptista thought that by the time it passed it would be dark.

"At least the Inn-Keeper seems very obliging," she said.

"I do not expect many travellers stay here," the Earl replied. "The town where Barnard is waiting for

us, and which I have found in the past has a first-class
Hotel, is only twelve miles away, and it will be in-
furiating if we cannot get there."

"I am quite happy."

Baptista smiled at the Earl as she spoke. She was
thinking that for her, wherever they might stay, it
was an adventure and an excitement she had not expected when she escaped from her father.

How could she have been so fortunate as to find
anyone like the Earl not only to carry her swiftly
away from a terrifying future but also to be so understanding and at the same time so kind?

Baptista had never been alone with a man before,
and although she had no idea what the wrong sort of
man might expect of her, she thought that if she had
travelled with someone unpleasant it would have been
disagreeable, or she might even have been in the company of a man who tried to kiss her.

She had never been kissed, but she had read in
one of the novels she had borrowed from the servants
at home—which would never have been allowed in
her father's Library—that gentlemen did attempt to
kiss pretty girls, who, if they were pure, fought violently against such advances.

"The Earl certainly does not wish to kiss me,"
Baptista told herself, and found herself wondering
what it would be like if he did.

The Proprietor's wife, a middle-aged woman who
seemed somewhat dour and by no means as pleasant
as her husband, showed Baptista upstairs before dinner.

By now she realised that she would not only wash
her hands in the bedroom but also be obliged to stay
the night in it.

The Inn was a small one, and there were only two
bedrooms on the first floor adjacent to each other, and
both were low-ceilinged and sparsely furnished.

"You can have which room you like, *Madame,*"
the Proprietor's wife said.

Baptista, looking first at one, then the other, saw
there was in one room a four-poster bed hung with

ñeedlework curtains that were faded yet must at one time have been beautiful.

As the Inn-Keeper's wife saw Baptista admiring them, she explained that her husband had bought the bed from a *Château* nearby whose contents had been sold.

Because it looked more imposing than the bed in the other room, which was much smaller and with only a headboard made of plain wood, Baptista left the more impressive bedroom for the Earl.

There were no carpets on the floor, only mats, but the wooden boards were clean and she hoped the mattresses were the same.

However, while they were eating dinner and finding it better than the Earl had anticipated, he said:

"You cannot trust the beds in these small Inns, and I have therefore told my servants to bring in all the rugs from the carriage, and I suggest you lie on one and cover yourself with another."

Baptista looked at him wide-eyed.

"Are you saying we should not undress?"

"I have no intention of doing so," the Earl replied, "and I think you might be sorry if you did."

Baptista gave a little shudder.

"I shall take your advice."

She drank another glass of wine at dinner, and after they had sat talking in front of the fire she realised that she was very sleepy.

She gave a stifled little yawn and the Earl smiled.

"Go to bed, Baptista," he said, "and, to make up for lost time, I want to start very early tomorrow morning, so you will not be able to sleep late."

"I will not do that," Baptista replied, "and I hope by tomorrow it will have stopped raining."

"I was looking out before dinner," the Earl told her. "The storm has passed and the rain is lessening. At the same time, I would not want to travel in the dark, and we will be safe here."

"Where are the servants going to sleep?"

"I have already discovered that there are very comfortable hay-lofts over the stables."

The Earl smiled as he added:

"As a matter of fact, I think they will doubtless find them more comfortable than the beds upstairs!"

"I think you are being needlessly censorious about our accommodation," Baptista said. "The Proprictor's wife, who I understand has been doing the cooking, has certainly done her best considering that she was not expecting visitors."

"That is true," the Earl agreed. "I will see that tomorrow they are fully recompensed for the effort they have made on our behalf."

His clothes had been dried and he had sat down to dinner wearing his jacket.

Despite being in riding-clothes he looked so handsome and attractive that Baptista wished she had her new gown to wear, rather than being arrayed only in her riding-habit, which she had worn all day.

However, she thought it was unnecessary to wear the coat and had come down to dinner dressed in her skirt and a thin white blouse that had been provided for her to wear with the habit.

It had a little bow at the neck and there was a frill at her waist, and she thought to herself that after the dull, drab clothes her father had made her wear, it was extremely elegant.

She had taken a great deal of trouble in arranging her hair, then thought despairingly that the Earl would find her neither smart nor attractive when he compared her with the ladies who entertained him in London and those who would be waiting for him in Paris.

Again, she was very ignorant of the circle in which the Earl moved, but she had often read the Social Columns in the newspapers.

The names of the people mentioned had meant nothing to her, but it had made her aware that there was a world of gaiety, amusement, Balls, and parties outside the walls of her home, which to all intents and purposes was a prison.

"Why cannot I attend a Ball, Papa?" she had asked her father one day.

She had not thought of the consequences of such an artless question and had brought down on her head a tirade against those who sought only a life of pleasure at the expense of their souls, and a violent denunciation of her wish to follow a life of sin which would lead to eternal damnation.

She had never asked her father such a question again, but she often thought how wonderful it would be to dance and to attend one of the Balls given in London which were reported the following day in the Society Columns of *The Times* and *The Morning Post*.

She knew now that the Earl's name must often have been amongst the long lists of guests, and she thought that she would in the future always look to see where he had been.

She could imagine him talking to some beautiful woman glittering with jewels or dancing with her under the crystal chandeliers in a crowded Ball-Room.

She wondered why the idea seemed to give her almost a pain in her heart and told herself there was no need to be envious.

She was sure that her mother would take her to Balls in Paris and that she would find plenty of young Frenchmen who wished to dance with her.

'They will not look like the Earl,' she thought wistfully.

She was certain that never again would she see a man who was so handsome or was such an outstanding rider.

As she went upstairs in the Inn she thought perhaps she was being foolish to leave the Earl so early when she might have gone on talking to him.

Then she knew that she was in fact very tired and it would spoil all the things they were going to do tomorrow if she was fatigued.

She found herself hoping that this delay would mean that they would not reach Paris as quickly as the Earl had intended.

"Once he deposits me with Mama," she told herself, "I will never see him again."

The thought made her feel that she must treasure

every second she was with him, and once again she had the impulse to go back down the stairs, sit in front of the fire, and go on talking to him.

Then she told herself he would very likely prefer to be alone, as he had told her to go to bed.

While they were dining the rugs from the carriage had been taken upstairs and Baptista now saw that on her bed was a woollen one to cover the bed-clothes and another lined with fur to cover her.

Although it was a warm night, the damp outside and inside the room made her shiver, and she hoped that the Earl would not be cold as she had obviously been given the thickest rugs.

Because he had told her to sleep in her clothes, she took off her blouse and washed in the basin which stood on a deal table at the side of the room.

That water was cold, but she did not mind that, though the towel, which was small and rough, made it difficult to dry herself.

She put on her blouse again, hoping it would not be too creased when morning came, and, taking off her shoes, sat down gingerly on the bed.

It seemed exceedingly comfortable and she suspected that the mattress was made of goose-feathers.

She had often heard that if not properly treated they attracted insects, and she knew that was why the Earl had no intention of sleeping inside the bed even if the sheets were clean.

She had found last night to her surprise that the Earl travelled with his own linen, and on Mr. Barnard's instructions a pair of his sheets had been arranged on the bed she had used.

She had not at first understood when the Courier had said:

"I hope you will be comfortable tonight, Miss Hawk. His Lordship always travels with every possible necessity, and fortunately there is enough to spare on this journey."

Then when she had seen the fine linen of the sheets and on them the beautifully embroidered monogram of the Earl, she had understood.

'I am sure this is something of which Papa would most vehemently disapprove,' she had thought with a little smile as she snuggled down comfortably and felt the softness of the linen against her cheek.

Tonight there was only the wool of the rug that covered the pillows provided by the Inn, but as Baptista shut her eyes she fell asleep almost immediately....

*   *   *

She awakened from a dream which vanished as she tried to remember what it had been about, and found that she felt very thirsty.

It must have been, she thought, one of the dishes at dinner which had been heavily spiced.

She wanted to go back to sleep, for she was still tired, but her thirst prevented her from doing so, and after a while she sat up and groped for the candle which stood on a table by the bed.

She managed with a little difficulty to light it, then stepped onto the floor in her stockinged feet and walked towards the basin where she had washed.

To her dismay, she found that there was no glass and no water except that in which she had washed, emptying the whole ewer into the basin to do so.

Her lips were dry, and, knowing it would be impossible to get back to sleep unless she could have something to drink, she walked across the room and very tentatively opened the door, expecting to find the Inn in darkness with nobody about.

To her surprise there were lights still burning at the bottom of the stairs, and it struck her that although she had been asleep it might still be early from the Inn-Keeper's point of view, and therefore she could ask for a glass of water to be brought upstairs to her by his wife.

She walked from the door of her bedroom to the top of the stairs and was just about to call out when she saw that down below, standing by the fire in front of which she and the Earl had sat earlier in the evening, the Inn-Keeper was talking to two men.

They were rough, coarse individuals and, Baptista thought, even dirtier than the man who had opened the door for her when she had first arrived.

She wondered if perhaps they were labourers employed by the Inn-Keeper. Then as she hesitated at the thought of drawing their attention to herself, she heard him say:

"He ought to be asleep by now. Be careful not to make a noise. We don't want the girl screaming."

It was not only what he said but the way he said it that made Baptista stiffen.

"Leave everything to us," answered one of the men to whom he was speaking. "There won't be no screaming, and no-one'll know anything till the morn'."

He spoke in such an argot that it was difficult for Baptista to understand what he was saying, and yet strangely enough his meaning was very clear.

"That's right," the Inn-Keeper said, "an' I know nothing! I was in bed asleep! And don't forget to break the window when you comes down, to show you broke in to get at him."

"You knows nothin'," the other man agreed, "and we'll be far away afore his servants ask you what they can do with the body."

"Don't forget to leave me my share!" the Inn-Keeper said sharply.

"You'll get it," the first man said, "and now let's get on with the job."

As he spoke he drew a long knife from his belt and Baptista saw that the other man carried a heavy club in his hand.

With a sudden jerk she realised what was happening and that she had stood listening to what the men were saying almost as if she were in a dream.

Swiftly but silently she stepped back from the head of the stairs and reached the door of the Earl's room, which was next to hers.

Her stockinged feet made no sound and she stepped inside and shut the door without making any noise.

She turned round when she had done so and saw

to her relief that the Earl had left a candle burning beside his bed, but he was asleep.

He was stretched out without having covered himself with a rug, and although he had taken off his coat he still wore his boots.

Baptista ran to his side and put her hand on his shoulder. At the same time, because she was afraid he would speak aloud to her when he awoke, she put her other hand over his mouth.

The Earl's eyes opened immediately, and as she felt his lips move as he tried to speak, she bent down to whisper in his ear:

"There are two men coming up the stairs to . . . kill and . . . rob you! What shall we . . . do? How can we . . . escape?"

The Earl sat up in bed.

"Two men, did you say?" he asked so quietly that it was difficult for her to hear him.

She nodded and looked round the room despairingly, thinking that they hardly had time to jump out the window even if it was feasible, and there was certainly nowhere to hide.

Then without asking any more questions the Earl got off the bed, and, taking Baptista by the arm, he pushed her across the room and behind a tall deal chest-of-drawers which was placed across one corner of the room.

"Keep down!" he ordered in a whisper.

She saw him glance towards the fireplace. The fire was unlit, but there were a few wooden logs in the grate and beside them was a stout iron poker.

The Earl picked it up, then to Baptista's surprise he blew out the candle.

Because she could not see him it made what was happening all the more terrifying.

Although he had moved very quietly she was sure he had walked towards the door, and now she waited, feeling as if her heart would burst in her breast, aware that someone outside was lifting the latch almost noiselessly and the door was opening very, very slowly.

There was a faint light which came from down below and she thought it probably came from the fire which might have been made up with extra logs.

The light widened as the door opened and it made what was happening seem even more sinister than it was already.

Baptista was so afraid that she thought at any moment her nerve might break and she would scream from sheer terror. But she knew she would endanger the Earl even more if the robbers were alerted to the fact that they were expected.

She therefore bit her lip and found that she could not even breathe as the door opened still farther, and now there was just the shadow of a body coming into the room.

Then like an evil signal there was a glint of light on the blade of the knife, which made Baptista clasp her fingers together in a sudden agony.

The man must have come one step farther, and as he did so the Earl brought the heavy poker down with a smashing blow on his wrist, which made him scream with pain.

Before he knew what was happening he had received a blow on his chin which knocked him to the floor, and before the man following could even raise his club, he too staggered under an upper-cut.

Before he could regain his balance he was hit again. Then as the Earl thrust him back against the bannisters on the landing at the top of the stairs, they cracked beneath his weight, and even before they could break, the Earl hit him for the third time and he crashed down onto the floor below.

By this time the first man on the floor was coming back to consciousness.

The Earl dragged him across the landing and with a derisive gesture threw him after his friend.

There was the sound of another heavy crash, then there was silence, and the Earl walked back into the bedroom, leaving the door open to give himself enough light to reach the candle.

Only when he had lit it did Baptista find she could breathe again, and with a little cry she came from behind the chest-of-drawers and ran across the room to fling herself against the Earl.

She was frantic with fear and trembling all over as she held on to him, but she realised he was smiling.

"It is all right," he said quietly. "They will not trouble us again."

"W-we cannot . . . stay here," she said in a voice she did not recognise as her own, "we must . . . go away . . . at once!"

"Why?" he asked.

He seemed so unperturbed that she felt her own agitation subsiding.

"W-why?" she repeated. "Because you might at this moment have been dead!"

"But I am not—thanks to you," the Earl replied. "If you are frightened of those gentlemen downstairs, I assure you, if they have not broken their arms or legs, which I hope they have, they will certainly not be in any condition to climb the stairs again."

He gave a little laugh as he said:

"I am really very grateful to you, Baptista. It is a long time since I have had to defend myself in such a manner, and I am very gratified to find that I am still able to do so."

"You were . . . wonderful!" Baptista said admiringly. "But . . . please . . . let us leave."

The Earl shook his head.

"The horses need a rest and so do the servants, and incidentally so do you. Go to bed, Baptista, I promise you there is no further danger."

She looked at him wide-eyed, then because she saw he meant what he said, she asked:

"Could I . . . please stay here . . . with you? I could not . . . bear to be . . . alone."

The Earl hesitated, then as if he was amused by the suggestion he said:

"Of course. I should be delighted for you to keep me company, and the bed is big enough for both of us and is actually quite comfortable."

As he spoke, he walked across the room to shut the door.

Then he looked at Baptista, who was standing

where he had left her, a little irresolute, afraid that he was annoyed because she had asked if she might stay with him.

As if he understood her hesitation, he said kindly but calmly:

"Of course I will look after you, Baptista. Lie down on the bed and try to sleep. Otherwise you will be too tired tomorrow to enjoy talking about this adventure as I am quite certain you will want to do."

There was a slightly mocking note in his voice which reassured her more than perhaps anything else could have done.

She gave an answering little laugh which sounded curiously like a sob as she said:

"I shall not ... want to ... talk about it because it is so ... frightening, but I find it ... hard to ... believe that you could ... vanquish those two ... horrible men so ... quickly and efficiently."

"Then you will agree that I have earned my sleep," the Earl said, "and if you snore, I shall insist that you return to your own room."

"I never snore!" Baptista replied indignantly.

The Earl went round to the other side of the bed.

He stretched himself out in the same way he had been lying when Baptista had come to wake him.

"Blow out the candle," he said, "and tomorrow you shall tell me how clever I have been. But at the moment it is too late for anything but pleasant dreams."

Because she knew she must obey him, Baptista blew out the candle as he had told her to do, then lowered herself carefully onto the bed beside him.

As she lay down she felt him pull the rug over her, and because she felt cold from the shock of what had happened she was glad of its warmth.

For a moment she was still and tense from what she thought was the most terrifying thing that had ever happened to her in her whole life.

Then she was suddenly aware that she was lying beside a man in the darkness and she was certain that it was something her father would think extremely reprehensible if not wicked.

'I cannot help it,' Baptista thought to herself. 'I could not ... bear to be alone ... and after all ... he is ... pretending that he is my ... uncle.'

Then as if the Earl was aware of what she was thinking he said:

"Stop worrying, Baptista, about robbers or anything else. Remember there will be exciting things to do tomorrow."

"I am so ... glad that you will be ... there to do ... them with ... me," Baptista answered.

Now there was no mistaking that there was a sob in her voice.

As she spoke she felt the Earl reach out and take her hand.

"I will be there," he said gently, "thanks to you, Baptista."

His fingers tightened, then she felt his lips hard, warm, and somehow insistent on her skin.

Chapter Four

Baptista heard somebody call her name and opened her eyes.

For a moment she could not think where she was, then she saw the Earl standing beside the bed.

"Wake up, Baptista!" he said. "I want to leave as soon as we have had breakfast."

As he spoke, everything that had happened the night before came to Baptista's mind and she gave a little cry and sat up on the bed.

"You are ... safe?" she asked. "Nothing ... happened when I was ... asleep?"

"No. I am quite safe," the Earl replied with a

smile, "and so are you. Hurry and get yourself ready. I have arranged for some hot water to be brought to your room."

He went from the bedroom as he spoke, and Baptista remembered that she had slept all night in her clothes and in consequence she felt hot and sticky.

She got out of bed thinking it strange that she had slept so peacefully with the Earl beside her.

Because she knew that he could deal with any robbers who might attack them, she had not worried or been afraid but had just shut her eyes and fallen asleep.

She felt in consequence quite clear-headed and ready to enjoy riding with the Earl.

She hurried next door to the bedroom she had chosen last night and thought how lucky it was that she had felt thirsty, otherwise the Earl at this moment might be lying dead and she herself would be in despair.

She could not imagine him dead, and she thought that if the robbers had carried out their wicked plan it would have been a most horrifying crime.

What was more, because the Police would be involved, they would doubtless have got in touch with her father.

She gave a little cry of terror at the idea, then hurriedly, pulling off her clothes, she washed in the water that the Earl had ordered for her.

It was only luke-warm, but she was in too much of a hurry to worry about anything except joining him again.

It was only when she had washed, dressed, and picked up the coat of her habit to put it over her arm that she wondered what would be waiting for them downstairs.

She thought she would never forget the manner in which the Earl had knocked the robbers unconscious. Then she heard the crash as they had fallen to the floor below.

The only evidence of it now was that the top of the bannisters was broken.

There were no bodies lying beneath the stairs,

and except for the fact that the Inn-Keeper served their breakfast in silence and with a shifty look in his eyes, there was nothing to show that they had done anything but pass a peaceful night in his Inn.

The eggs, which Baptista knew the Earl had demanded English-fashion, were fresh, and the coffee, although not of the best quality, was drinkable.

"If you are still hungry," the Earl remarked, "we will have another breakfast when we arrive at the Hotel at which we should have stayed last night."

He spoke in English, knowing that the Inn-Keeper would not understand anything but his own language, and Baptista asked in a low voice:

"Did you say anything about what happened?"

"I think he would have a good idea of that without my bothering to put it into words," the Earl said with a smile, "and my servants have already told me that they saw two men being carried from the building very early this morning."

"Carried?" Baptista asked.

"They thought that one man had a broken leg, and the other was also unable to walk unaided."

"I am glad," Baptista said. "They deserve all the punishment they get!"

She spoke impulsively, then as if the word "punishment" recalled all too vividly her father and his desire for sinners to suffer, she flushed and went on with her breakfast without saying any more.

The Earl's eyes were on her face for a moment, then he rose to pay the bill and walked outside to see if the carriage was ready.

He had anticipated that Baptista would wish to ride with him and therefore the outriders were not mounted but were waiting to help her into the saddle.

She saw the footmen carry the rugs on which they had slept from the Inn to place them in the carriage, then she picked up her reins, the Earl rode ahead out of the courtyard, and she followed him.

As she galloped over the fields Baptista felt the pale morning sun and the freshness of the air sweep away the terrors of the night.

The heavy rain had left the ground damp and

muddy, but there was the scent of fresh grass which seemed to carry with it the fragrance of spring.

They rode for some time in silence. Then as the horses settled down to a trot the Earl said, almost as if she had been talking of the night before:

"I suggest you forget it. It is something that might never happen again in a thousand years, and you are very unlikely ever again to stay in such a squalid Inn."

"I am only feeling grateful that because I was thirsty I went to the top of the stairs to find ... something to ... drink."

"So that is how you heard what was being planned!"

"I was just going to call out and ask the Inn-Keeper's wife to bring me a glass of water, then I heard what the men were ... saying."

"I must commend you on your knowledge of French."

"Mama was very insistent that I should speak other languages besides my own. Perhaps she had a presentiment that it might save me ... and you."

"Whatever the reason, "I am very grateful," the Earl said. "And now, as I have already said, let us forget anything so unpleasant and look forward to what lies ahead."

As he spoke he knew there was a question-mark over that as far as Baptista was concerned.

Last night when he had lain awake listening to her quiet breathing, it had struck him that it was her innocence that had made her accept quite naturally that she should lie beside him on his bed.

He had an unusual understanding of what Baptista felt, and he knew that the reason why she was not embarrassed was that they were neither of them undressed. Moreover, she was not yet actually aware of him as a man, so she was not afraid.

It struck the Earl that the danger in store for Baptista was not merely that of being robbed.

He wondered how many men of his acquaintance, let alone the type of Frenchman she might have encountered on the road, would have let her sleep for the rest of the night as quietly as a child.

When the dawn broke and the first rays of the sun came through the uncurtained windows the Earl had seen Baptista's face near to his.

She looked very young cuddled down into the rug he had tucked round her, and her eye-lashes were dark against the whiteness of her skin.

He saw that they curled back and were pale gold at the roots and darkened naturally at the ends.

Her hair had become a little loosened while she had slept and there were small golden curls against her oval forehead.

"She is very lovely," the Earl had told himself.

Then once again he was worrying as to what would happen to her when she reached Paris.

He found himself remembering the parties he had attended in the house of La Paiva and those given by other *Grandes Cocottes.*

Their exotic entertainments were the talk of Europe, and he recalled one given by Cora Pearl when the floor was sprinkled with orchids, costing thousands of francs, on which she danced.

Another party which had interested him much more had been arranged by Madame Musard, who was the mistress of the King of the Netherlands, to whom she owed her vast wealth.

The guests all assembled in a long Gallery draped with green curtains. Breakfast, which included truffles and champagne, had been served and eaten and coffee and cigars had followed. Then unexpectedly a bell was rung and the draperies were swept away.

The Gallery had become a stable where stood eighteen magnificent horses, which had also breakfasted.

The Earl remembered how they had all laughed and commended Madame Musard on having an original idea, but other parties which he had attended on other visits had by the end of the evening become orgies.

They undoubtedly amused him and the other

gentlemen who were present, but they were certainly not the sort of entertainments at which he would have liked to see Baptista.

"I need not trouble myself," he decided. "Her mother will look after her."

Yet once again he found himself questioning the sort of life her mother would lead as the mistress of the *Comte* de Saucorne.

An hour later they entered the town where they should have stayed the night and found Mr. Barnard waiting for them at the Hotel, extremely perturbed as to what might have happened.

"The storm made it impossible for us to continue our journey," the Earl said briefly, "and we were forced to stay at a most undesirable Inn. What we require now, Barnard, are baths, a change of clothing, and after that an early luncheon."

"That is what I expected you would ask for, My Lord," Mr. Barnard replied, "and everything is in readiness in a Suite on the first floor."

He escorted them up the stairs and Baptista found that there was a maid to wait on her, and there was not only a bath in which she felt she could soak away the discomforts as well as the horrors of last night but also a surprise when she was ready to dress.

Mr. Barnard had filled in the time he was waiting by purchasing her another riding-habit, an even smarter one than he had been able to procure for her before.

There was also a gown for the evening and another for the day, so attractive and so different from anything she had ever owned that Baptista could have cried for sheer joy when she saw them.

When she went into the Sitting-Room for breakfast she had put on her riding-habit which was of green silk trimmed with white braid.

The Earl was waiting for her and she ran towards him to say excitedly:

"Thank you, thank you! I am sure it was you who told Mr. Barnard to buy some more clothes for me. I do hope that tonight we shall dine somewhere smart so that I can wear my evening-gown."

The Earl smiled.

"We are having an easy day. I have already arranged to stay at Chantilly, where there is an excellent Hotel, and perhaps as a treat, so that you can have an audience, we will dine in the Restaurant."

Baptista clasped her hands together excitedly.

"I would love that because I have never been in a Restaurant," she said.

The Earl thought with a little smile of amusement that most women of his acquaintance would be much more anxious to dine alone with him in his private Sitting-Room.

He knew that Baptista, having been so constrained while she lived with her father, was like a child who found that anything new carried her into what was a fairy-land of delight.

He had told himself so often that he liked only sophisticated women like Lady Marlene to amuse him, but now, because for Baptista everything was new, he found himself watching her joy over things that to him were too commonplace even to notice.

She liked the flowers, the silk cushions, and even the decorations in the Sitting-Room.

"I had no idea a Hotel could be as luxurious as this!" she exclaimed. "I had always thought them to be more like the one in which we stayed last night."

She peeped into his bedroom to see if it was different from hers, then she enjoyed every dish that was presented to them at luncheon.

"I did not know food could taste so delicious," she answered. "Do you always eat like this?"

"Only in France," the Earl replied, "although my Chef at Hawk is excellent. I think one should always enjoy the food of the country in which one finds oneself."

Baptista gave a little laugh.

"That means roast beef in England and frogs'-legs in France."

"I have not offered you any yet," the Earl replied.

Baptista wrinkled her nose.

"I have read about them and I am sure they taste horrid!"

"They taste like young chicken," the Earl said, "but we will wait until you are more acclimatised before I give you frogs'-legs or snails."

There was silence, then Baptista said in a small voice:

"When will we ... arrive in Paris?"

"We should have been there tonight, but because we are staying at Chantilly we will get there tomorrow afternoon."

He saw the expression on Baptista's face and said quietly:

"I am going to take you first to stay with my friend the *Vicomte* de Dijon, then I will start looking for your mother."

He saw a sudden light in Baptista's eyes and once again he knew perceptively that she was thinking perhaps it might take some time for him to find her mother.

He rose from the table, saying abruptly:

"I think we should be on our way."

As he went downstairs into the Hall ahead of Baptista, he told himself that she was growing attached to him, doubtless only because she looked to him to protect and take care of her. Nevertheless, such an attitude must not go too far.

The Earl thought that since she was so young it was very unlikely that she would fall in love with him, but he must try to prevent such a thing from happening because he had no wish to hurt her.

She was little more than a child, and he was the first man who had ever come into her life. It was therefore understandable that she would wish to cling to him, especially when they had spent such an eventful time together.

But the truth was that the sooner he found her mother and she was no longer on his hands, the better.

He was also very certain that he did not wish to become embroiled in any way with Lord Dunsford.

There was no doubt that the man was mad and somebody should take him to task for the way in which he treated his daughter. But the Earl was determined that it would not be his job to do so.

'I told myself when I left England,' he thought, 'that I would not become involved with any more women, and here I am in a situation which could become extremely uncomfortable for me unless I am careful.'

It flashed through his mind that he had been stupid in staying the night at Chantilly instead of pushing on to Paris.

But actually it was too far a distance for his horses as well as for Baptista, and they were more important to him than she was.

The Earl told himself that what he would do was to give Baptista dinner in the Restaurant, then send her to bed.

'Barnard can find out if there are any amusements for me in Chantilly,' he thought.

Since it was so near to Paris and there were a number of important *Châteaux* near the town, he was quite certain that what the French aristocrats expected in the way of amusement would not have been neglected.

"What I want is what I am used to!" the Earl said positively.

Then he found himself admiring the picture Baptista made in her new green habit as she rode a black stallion which he thought was one of the most magnificent-looking horses in his stable.

The Hotel at Chantilly was a delight to Baptista, and the Earl found his conviction that to him all Hotels were uninteresting being swept away by her enthusiasm.

Newly decorated, their Suite overlooked a garden and the beds were draped with frilled muslin curtains that were the *dernier cri* in French Hotels.

"It is so pretty and so comfortable," Baptista kept saying.

She was entranced by the chambermaids, who wore pink cotton dresses with lace-trimmed caps and aprons.

When she was dressed for dinner in the new gown that Mr. Barnard had provided for her, she stared in the mirror, thinking she was seeing not herself but some strange and very attractive young woman.

The gown which Mr. Barnard had chosen with unerring taste, because it matched her eyes, was made in the very elaborate style which the Empress had brought into fashion.

The bustle was a cascade of frills and there were bunches of small roses to decorate the draped skirt.

To Baptista it was a revelation after years of being deprived even of a sash to her gowns.

The maid who was looking after her, also infected by her excitement, had arranged her hair in the new fashion which gave her little ringlets of curls falling from the back of her head onto her shoulders.

'I am sure the Earl will admire me when I look like this,' Baptista thought.

She wondered what she would do to amuse him, as the ladies he usually dined with would contrive to do.

"I expect they will flirt with him," she told herself, and wondered exactly what flirting meant.

Then, because it was a waste of time to stand looking at herself when she might be with the Earl, she hurried to the Sitting-Room where she knew he would be waiting for her.

She was not mistaken, and when she entered he was standing in front of the marble fireplace, drinking a glass of champagne.

As she had done with the first gown he had given her, she stood still dramatically in the doorway, holding out her arms so that he could look at her.

The Earl was aware immediately that the gown was quite an admirable effort on Barnard's part, but it was hard to look at anything except the excitement in Baptista's face, the blue of her eyes, and the smile on her lips.

He did not speak, and as if she could not bear the suspense she ran towards him.

"Tell me what you think ... tell me!" she insisted.

"About what?" he teased.

For a second her smile vanished. Then as she saw the expression in his eyes, she said:

"Do you think I am pretty really . . . pretty enough to dine with you as if I were a . . . lovely lady you had invited to a *tête-à-tête?*"

The Earl sensed there was a little anxiety behind the question, and he answered sincerely:

"You look very lovely and I am very honoured that we should, as you put it, have a *tête-à-tête.*"

Baptista gave a little skip for joy.

"That is what I wanted you to say, and I have never in my whole life worn such a lovely gown or thought I should own one."

"I am glad it pleases you."

"Pleases me?" Baptista echoed. "I want never to take it off—except if I had to sleep in it like last night, I might spoil it."

"That is certainly not something you will have to do tonight," the Earl said. "May I give you a glass of champagne?"

Baptista shook her head.

"I think it would be a mistake. I am too excited already, and if I drink champagne I might sing for joy or dance on the table. Then you would be ashamed of me."

"I certainly would!" the Earl said firmly.

"In a book I once read, the heroine did just that, and the hero, maddened by her beauty, carried her away into the night."

"I cannot think your father approved of that sort of reading," the Earl said.

"Papa did not know, and the novel was lent to me by one of our housemaids. She was better educated than most of them, and because one of Papa's friends told him so, he dismissed her."

"Why should he do that?" the Earl asked in surprise.

"He said that no woman, especially those in the lower classes, should have brains, that they were unsettling and made them discontented with their lot."

"He allowed you to be educated."

"Mama insisted on it, but I think Papa might have stopped it after she left, except that I had to have a Governess with me as a companion."

"And she was intelligent enough to teach you what you wanted to know?"

"She was a very clever woman ... clever enough to realise that Papa must not think her anything but stupid."

The Earl laughed.

"So even your father was deceived by the wiles of Eve?"

"She stayed with me even though the house was so gloomy and depressing, and I am sure she would have been happier somewhere else. But she loved me."

"And now you are one of those most regrettable creatures—a clever woman."

"I wish I were," Baptista answered, "but the truth is that I know how ignorant I am and how little I know about anything except a few books."

She spoke regretfully, then a smile lit up her face.

"Now I shall learn lots about everything in Paris, and that is an exciting thought in itself."

"It depends on what you want to learn," the Earl said cautiously.

"Of course I am interested in the buildings, the Churches, and the Seine," Baptista began.

She paused, then continued:

"But most of all I want to see and meet the people. I want to see not only what they look like but find out what they think and feel, and I am sure that is the real way to learn about other countries."

The Earl wanted to say again that it depended on what sort of people she met, but he thought it would be difficult to explain, so instead he suggested that they go downstairs to dinner.

Baptista was very impressed with the Dining-Room, which had red walls ornamented with mirrors and red velvet chairs which matched the heavily fringed curtains of the same colour.

"It is very grand!" she said almost in a whisper to the Earl after they had been shown to the best table in the room.

"I thought it would amuse you."

He had already ordered dinner before they went

downstairs, and the first course was brought almost immediately and also the wine which the Earl had chosen as a knowledgeable epicure.

"Tell me what are the best Restaurants in Paris," Baptista asked as they began to eat.

The Earl described two places where he had eaten superlative meals and Baptista listened attentively. Then she said:

"After you have found Mama for me, will I ever ... see you ... again?"

"I hope so," the Earl replied. "I often have to come to Paris and I shall certainly be interested to find out if you are happy."

Even to himself his voice sounded almost too casual and he was aware that the light had gone out of Baptista's eyes.

There was silence for a moment, then she said:

"Supposing Mama does not ... want me? What ... shall I do ... then?"

It was a question the Earl had already asked himself and found no answer.

"What have you considered doing?" he asked evasively.

"I do not know. I cannot go back to England because of Papa, so I would have to stay in Paris. But I am not certain that it would be possible for me to get hold of any of my money ..."

Her voice died away and after a moment she said:

"You were saying just now that I was well educated, but I cannot think that I have learnt anything that would earn me any money."

She looked at him a little despairingly and the Earl found himself thinking that a Frenchman would answer that question very easily, and because the thought was unwelcome it annoyed him.

"Surely it is quite unnecessary to worry ourselves tonight with questions over hypothetical problems which may not arise?" he asked. "Let us assume that your mother will be delighted to see you and you can live with her, so that there will be no difficulties in the future."

"That is what I hope will happen," Baptista replied. "At the same time, when you leave me there will be no-one to turn to if I am in trouble."

"You must have been aware of that when you ran away from your father," the Earl said. "After all, it was just by chance that I came into your life, and we have in fact only a very slight acquaintance with each other."

As he spoke he knew that to Baptista it was more than that.

He had not only felt desperately sorry for her for having Lord Dunsford as a father, but they had also shared an experience of danger which had, in a way, drawn them closer to each other than they would have been if they had just met at parties or Balls.

He found himself thinking how she had lain down beside him and fallen asleep, confident that he would protect her and keep her safe until daylight.

'She is so young and trusting,' the Earl thought. 'What will happen to her in Paris?'

"You are looking fierce and rather grim," Baptista said accusingly.

The Earl forced a smile to his lips.

"Then I must apologise. That is certainly not the way to behave when dining with a lovely lady."

"When you are with one of the ladies you usually dine with," Baptista asked, "what do you talk about?"

The Earl certainly knew the answer to that.

They would be talking about themselves, and his dinner-companion would be using every allure in her repertoire to entice and excite him.

"What do you think we talk about?" he asked.

"I was thinking when I was dressing," Baptista replied, "that a lady wearing a gown like this would want to flirt with you. The trouble is, I do not know how to flirt or what one says or does."

The Earl did not answer and she bent towards him across the table.

"Please tell me what I should do," she said, "then perhaps I shall be a ... sensation when I get to Paris and Mama will be ... pleased with me."

The idea suddenly annoyed the Earl unreasonably.

"You are far too young to flirt, as you call it," he said sharply, "or to spoil yourself by being anything but natural."

She looked surprised at the way he had spoken, and she said humbly:

"I only want to improve myself, and I want... you to... admire me, and not find me a ... bore."

"I should certainly find you a bore if you pretended to be anything you were not or deliberately tried to attract men."

He might have guessed that this statement would arouse Baptista's interest.

"Do you mean that women know how to make a man think they are attractive?" she asked. "Is it something they say, the way they look, or what they do?"

"I really have no idea," he said quickly.

"I do not think that is true," Baptista answered. "I am sure, when I think about it, that if a woman wants to attract a man, she can approach him in some special way, or perhaps say things to him that make him want to... carry her away into the night, or... perhaps... kiss her."

The Earl was silent, thinking this was a very strange conversation and one which he should avoid, but he was not quite certain how he could do so.

Baptista looked at him reflectively.

"Do you think... and please tell me the truth, that men will want to kiss me? Would... you like to... kiss me?"

The Earl's eyes met hers, then quickly he looked away.

"I think we have both forgotten," he said, "that you are my niece and this is not the sort of conversation you would be having with your uncle."

"I wish I had a dozen uncles like you," Baptista said, "but I am certain that if Papa had a brother he would be like him and I would have had two of them scolding and beating me, and that would be too frightening even to contemplate!"

"Nevertheless," the Earl said, "you are well aware how you should behave as my niece, and as we shall be in Paris tomorrow, you had better start practising. So we will talk of something quite different."

"You might have just answered my question," Baptista said. "I shall find myself worrying about it, and I am sure that when you kiss a lovely lady, it is very . . . very exciting for . . . her."

The Earl did not miss the almost pathetic note of wistfulness in her voice.

He knew, although it seemed incredible, that she was thinking that nobody would want to kiss her, especially as all the time they had been alone together he had shown no inclination to do so.

It suddenly struck him that something he had never done before was to awaken a young girl to womanhood.

The first kiss he had ever given had been to a woman much older than himself, and when he had looked back he had been able to see that she had been attracted by him and had deliberately set out to ensnare him.

He was sure that Baptista's lips would be very soft, very sweet, and very innocent, and he felt a sudden desire to reassure her that she was extremely attractive and to be the first man to make her aware of it.

Then he told himself it would be very reprehensible: the child trusted him, and to abuse that trust in any way would be both wrong and unsporting.

At the same time, he could not help thinking that any other man in the same position, especially the type of men she would meet after tomorrow, would not fail to accept what fate had brought them in the shape of a girl both pure and unspoilt in a manner that was almost unique in the world today.

Fortunately, at that moment more food was brought to the table, which diverted Baptista's attention.

It was only when dinner was finished, and coffee and a glass of brandy for the Earl had been left on the table, that she said with a smile:

"Now we can go on talking, and please try to help

me to be more knowledgeable, otherwise I am afraid people will laugh at me when I reach Paris."

"Why should you think they will do that?"

"Because I shall make gaffes and say stupid things simply because I am ignorant."

"If when you first arrive you keep very quiet, you will soon learn from other people's behaviour what is expected of you."

As he spoke, he hoped the advice he was giving her was good.

But once again there were a number of question-marks as to what sort of people she would meet and what their behaviour would be, and certainly there was a doubt as to whether she would understand the *double entendres* of ordinary French conversation.

"I suppose really," Baptista said, "I am feeling afraid because I shall have to leave you. You said we were just acquaintances, but I feel as if I have known you all my life and you have always been there in my mind."

"I wonder why you should feel like that," the Earl remarked. "Perhaps it is because you have not met many people, living at home with your father."

"That is what I expected you would say," she answered, "but it is more than that. At first I thought you were so important, so overwhelming, and I was completely insignificant and of no consequence beside you."

She paused and was obviously feeling for words before she continued:

"Then I began to feel that in a way I was almost a part of you. I could understand what you were thinking, and I know you understand my thoughts, because sometimes you answer them without my even saying them aloud. Why do we feel like that?"

"Why do *you* feel like that?" the Earl questioned.

"I do not know the answer," Baptista replied. "But what do you feel about me?"

The Earl chose his words with care.

"I think you are a very attractive, very charming young girl who needs a mother or a father to look after her until she finds the right man to marry."

"That, I suppose, is what every girl wants," Baptista agreed. "But most of all they want a home, which is something I do not possess."

It was typical, because she was so sharp-brained, that she should put her finger unerringly on the point he had felt obliged to omit.

"We none of us find perfection in this world," he answered, "and therefore we have to make do with what we have. When you find your mother, Baptista, or rather I find her for you, then you can just enjoy yourself for a year or so until you find a husband."

"If I get married," Baptista answered, "I would want to be in love as Mama was in love when she ran away with the *Comte*. I should also want a man who could ride as well as you and be as clever as you."

"You are very complimentary," the Earl said drily.

"I would not ask that he be as handsome as you," Baptista went on, as if he had not spoken, "because I think that would be impossible, but I could not bear to marry a man who is stupid or who could not handle a horse."

"I am sure you will find plenty of men with those qualifications."

"There is . . . something else as . . . well."

"That is that?"

"If I were to . . . marry a man, he would have to be kind . . ."

She paused and the Earl knew what she was going to say.

"Papa was unkind and cruel, but you are kind," Baptista went on. "You were kind when you helped me to escape when you did not really want to. You have been kind in letting me ride with you and in buying me these wonderful clothes, and most of all in bringing me as far as Paris when you really wished to be rid of me at the first town we came to."

"That was before I knew you," the Earl said.

"I realise it will be embarrassing for you to pretend to your friends that I am your niece," Baptista said, "and perhaps, because I am so grateful for all you have . . . done for me . . . I should stay in a cheap Hotel or Lodging House until you can find Mama."

She lowered her voice before she added:

"I could not ... bear to hurt you in ... any way after all you have ... done for me."

"You are thinking of me, Baptista?"

"Of course I am thinking of you," she replied. "There is no man in the world who would be so kind ... or so ... wonderful."

There was a little sob on the last word, and as the Earl looked at Baptista incredulously, his eyes met hers, then it was impossible for either of them to look away.

It seemed to the Earl as if he looked through her blue eyes deep into her very soul, and he knew in spite of her intelligence how unsure and afraid she was, and yet she was not thinking of herself but of him.

He made a conscious effort to look away from her.

"We have already decided what we are going to do," he said, "and there is no point in arguing about it any further. The *Vicomte* de Dijon has never met my sisters and has no idea of the ages of their children. You will stay with him as my niece, and, if you wish to please me, you will not say anything which might make him doubt our relationship."

Baptista did not speak for a moment and he had the feeling that she was thinking about something else.

Then she said in a low voice that he could barely hear:

"I will do ... anything you ask ... but please ... please ... help me ... I shall be so ... afraid unless you ... do so."

Chapter Five

It was growing late in the evening when they drove into Paris, and Baptista was tremendously excited by all she saw.

"Look at the tall houses with their grey shutters!" she cried. "And the trees in every street. It is so pretty so... exactly what I thought Paris would be like!"

The Earl smiled at her enthusiasm.

Because he had wanted her to look her best, they had not ridden after they left Chantilly, but had driven in the carriage, and he thought the new gown Barnard had bought her was exceedingly becoming, as was the small bonnet that went with it, which was trimmed with flowers.

He had known that the clothes meant more to her than they would have done to a girl who had not been kept in a puritan state of austerity and never allowed the frivolities which meant so much to a woman.

Even so, he knew that few women of his acquaintance would have been so sincerely grateful instead of taking everything that was given to them as a right because they were beautiful.

He was aware that Baptista was not only unsure of her behaviour and her looks but also of her relationship to other people.

This was understandable, considering that she had been kept imprisoned in her father's house and both men and women of her own age were an unknown quantity.

He knew as they entered Paris that while she was thrilled with everything she saw, she was also apprehensive of meeting his friends and of no longer being alone with him.

"What is your friend the *Vicomte* like?" she had asked while they were having luncheon.

"He is a very charming and sophisticated Frenchman," the Earl answered without really thinking.

When he saw that this meant very little to Baptista, he explained further:

"The *Vicomte* is the eldest son of the *Marquis* St. Quentin, who is an extremely rich man, but in ill health, so he seldom leaves his magnificent *Château* in the Loire."

"I would like to see a really important *Château*," Baptista murmured.

The Earl continued as if she had not spoken:

"My friend the *Vicomte* therefore has the family house in Paris to himself, and you will find it holds some very interesting paintings as well as magnificent Louis XIV furniture which was luckily not destroyed in the Revolution."

He knew that Baptista was interested, and he went on:

"The *Vicomte* was married when he was very young, and his wife gave him two sons before she died giving birth to a third."

"I did not think of him as being married!" Baptista exclaimed. "I thought he would be a bachelor like you."

The Earl smiled.

"That is what he is, to all intents and purposes, because he leaves his children with their grandparents and enjoys himself in Paris."

There was a little silence, then Baptista said:

"And that is what you ... will do ... with him?"

He knew she was thinking once again of the women she called "lovely ladies," and he thought apprehensively that she had come very close to the truth.

"I have other things to do as well," he said evasively.

He remembered that it was what she had sus-

pected when she had said she was sure his journey
to Paris was not only in search of amusement.

There was silence, then she asked:

"Will you take me ... anywhere with you ... or
will you wish to go alone?"

It was a question the Earl had already asked himself, thinking it might add further to his indiscretion
in taking her from her father if she was seen at the
social gatherings to which inevitably he would be
asked on his arrival.

"I think the first thing we must do," he said
aloud, "is to try to find your mother, and of course
while we are doing so I will introduce you to some
of my French friends."

He thought to himself that he would choose them
very carefully, but he saw Baptista's eyes light up.
Then she said:

"Will my gowns be smart enough?"

The Earl laughed.

"There speaks the eternal Eve, who I am quite
certain never had enough fig-leaves! Let me tell you,
Baptista, I should be delighted in my role as uncle to
provide you with some Parisian gowns."

"I promise I will pay you back as soon as I can
handle any of my own money," Baptista said, "and I
expect Mama will pay for me if I am unable to do so
myself."

"I do not think you will bankrupt me," the Earl
said with a smile.

"You are so kind," Baptista said, "but I do not
want you to be ashamed of me, as you might be if
your French friends thought I looked dowdy."

The Earl thought that would be impossible, but
he merely said drily:

"That is something we must definitely prevent
from happening."

They drove on, and when they passed through
the Place de la Concorde, Baptista was even more excited than she had been before.

"I knew it would look like this," she said. "The
fountains make the whole place like a fairy-land. In

fact, because Paris is so beautiful I feel the French people who live in it will be beautiful too."

The Earl hoped a little cynically that she would continue to think so.

Then they were driving up the Champs Élysées and through the gold-tipped wrought-iron gates which led to the house where they would be staying.

Servants in very elaborate livery hurried to open the door of the carriage, and a splendidly garbed Major-Domo greeted them on behalf of his master and with a show of pomp and ceremony led them towards the Salon.

The Major-Domo halted to ask Baptista's name, and when the Earl had given it he flung the doors open with a dramatic gesture and announced:

"*Milord* Hawkshead and the Honourable *Mademoiselle* Hawk, *Monsieur le Vicomte!*"

The *Vicomte*, who had been reading the newspapers at the far end of the room, jumped to his feet and the Earl saw an expression of surprise on his face as he walked towards him holding out his hand.

"Irvin, I am delighted to see you!" he said in English. "I was expecting you yesterday."

"I am late owing to a storm," the Earl explained, "but I am glad to be here, Pierre, and I only hope that you will forgive me for bringing you an extra guest—my niece!"

The *Vicomte* held out his hand to Baptista, saying:

"Any relative of yours, Irvin, is extremely welcome, especially one who is so pretty!"

Baptista smiled, showing her dimples as she curtseyed.

"Baptista was unfortunately involved in an accident outside Calais," the Earl explained, "and I luckily arrived at just the right moment to rescue her."

"As far as I am concerned, it could not be more fortunate," the *Vicomte* said.

There was no mistaking the admiration in his eyes as he looked at Baptista.

"I have a glass of champagne waiting for you," he

added, "and I hope *Mademoiselle* will join us, unless there is something else she prefers?"

"I feel, as Paris is so lovely, that I should drink a toast to it," Baptista said.

"And we will toast you, *Mademoiselle*, because you will undoubtedly make Paris much more lovely than it is already."

The Earl noticed that Baptista seemed delighted with his compliments and, to his surprise, not embarrassed by them.

The *Vicomte* poured the champagne into their glasses, then raised his glass and said, looking at Baptista:

"To a new beauty who will, I know, eclipse all those who are dazzling Paris at the moment and give us all a new conception of loveliness!"

The words sounded very flattering in French, and the Earl thought a little sourly that if this continued Baptista would soon get her head turned.

"If you will excuse me," the *Vicomte* said, "I will just go and instruct my servants as to where your niece is to sleep."

"Please ... I would like ... if possible, to be near to my U-Uncle," Baptista said hesitatingly.

She stumbled over the word "Uncle" but the Earl thought his friend would not attach any particular significance to it.

"But of course," the *Vicomte* agreed, "I had already thought of that myself, as I know it is always frightening to be in a strange place."

"Thank you," Baptista said.

He smiled at her and went from the room, and Baptista said in a low voice:

"He is so exactly what I expected a French aristocrat to look like, but I feel as if I were taking part in a play."

The Earl understood why his friend's compliments had not embarrassed her.

"I should hardly have thought you were ever allowed to go to the Theatre," he said.

"No, of course not! Papa thought they were the haunts of Satan! But Miss Cunningham, my Governess, and I used to act Shakespeare's plays together, each taking different parts, and she showed me pictures of Play-Houses so I know what they look like and even how the scenery works."

The Earl laughed.

"And now you think that 'All the world's a stage, and all the men and women merely players,'" he quoted.

"At the moment I am the heroine," Baptista said, "and naturally you are the hero."

"I rather thought you were allotting that role to the *Vicomte!*"

Baptista shook her head, but before she could answer, their host returned.

A little while later they went upstairs to change for dinner.

Baptista was delighted with her bedroom, which had a painted ceiling rioting with goddesses and cupids, an Aubusson carpet with pink roses and blue ribbons woven into it, and the bed was draped with blue silk curtains suspended from a golden corolla.

"It is more beautiful than I could possibly imagine!" she cried excitedly.

"I am delighted it pleases you," the *Vicomte* answered, "and I can only say somewhat inadequately that it is the perfect background for someone who looks as if she has just stepped down from Olympus to dazzle mere humans like myself!"

The Earl knew that Baptista glanced at him swiftly as if they shared a secret, and once again he saw her dimples.

As he reached his own bedroom, where everything had already been unpacked, the *Vicomte* said:

"She is entrancing, Irvin! I had no idea you had such a lovely niece, but then everything you possess is superlative!"

"Baptista is very young," the Earl said repressively, "and I am only hoping that Paris will not spoil her."

"Every man she meets will fall at her feet," the *Vicomte* replied, "and although she is obviously very young, she has to grow up sometime."

"But not too quickly!" the Earl said sharply.

"Now you are sounding exactly like the type of relation who always wishes to prevent the young from enjoying themselves," the *Vicomte* teased. "I would not have expected that of you, Irvin."

"As I have just said, Baptista is very young, and while she is with me I intend to be very careful whom she meets."

"Nonsense! Let the child have a good time! And now that I think of it, my cousin is giving a small dance this evening for her daughter who is about the same age. I intended when you arrived that we should look for our amusement in a very different direction, but I think your niece would enjoy the party so we must take her to it."

The Earl hesitated, but because he thought it would seem strange if he refused what would obviously be the sort of party that Baptista would enjoy, he said grudgingly:

"Very well, but because she has been travelling for some time, she must not stay up too late."

The *Vicomte* looked at him in surprise. Then he said:

"I understand what you are saying, Irvin, therefore we will bring your niece home soon after midnight, which will leave us free to enjoy ourselves, as we have always done, with *les Grandes Cocottes.*"

He waited for the Earl to agree, and when he did not do so, he went on:

"La Paiva will undoubtedly be pleased to see you, and I believe La Castiglione has a party this evening. She still holds the Emperor's interest, by the way, and although he has found several other diversions, he always seems to return to her."

"I wonder why," the Earl remarked laconically. "I always thought her beautiful but extremely dull."

"Maybe she has hidden qualities we have not sampled," the *Vicomte* answered with a laugh.

He was just about to leave the room when the Earl said:

"By the way, Pierre, do you happen to know where I can find the *Comte* de Saucorne?"

"Jacques?" the *Vicomte* questioned. "If you wish to see him you have come at the right time to congratulate him. His wife has just presented him with an heir!"

"His wife?" the Earl repeated.

"Yes, Jacques was married a year ago."

"To whom?"

"It was an excellent match. The Saucornes, as you know, are a very old and respected family, but none too wealthy, while the daughter of the late *Comte* de Vence is a great heiress."

"And they were married a year ago?" the Earl asked.

"That is right," the *Vicomte* agreed. "Why are you so interested? I did not know you knew the Saucornes."

"I do not," the Earl answered, "but I understood he was living with an Englishwoman and I have a message for her from a friend of hers."

"As I understand it, you are talking of Marie-Louise."

The Earl looked puzzled and the *Vicomte* explained:

"Jacques returned to Paris some years ago with a fascinating creature whom I think he would have married if she had been free to do so. Her Christian name was Mary and when she and Jacques parted she changed it to Marie-Louise."

"Why did she do that?"

"I am curious as to why it interests you so much."

"I have told you," the Earl answered, "I have a message for her from a friend. I promised to give it to her, and, as you know, I always keep my promises."

"Is that all? I thought perhaps she might have been an old flame of yours."

"I have never met her," the Earl said crisply.

"What a pity! It would amuse me to see your reaction to how she looks now."

The Earl frowned.

"I wish you would not go on talking in riddles but tell me what I want to know. Where can I find this lady who you tell me is now called Marie-Louise?"

"She is at the moment the mistress of the Foreign Secretary, the *Duc* de Gramont!"

The Earl stiffened.

He thought as he spoke that it was extraordinary that while he had come to Paris to see and find out things about the *Duc,* he should be intimately connected with Baptista's mother, whom he was also seeking.

"Why did Marie-Louise, as she is called now, leave de Saucorne?" he asked.

"They were inseparable when they first arrived in Paris," the *Vicomte* replied, "and naturally Jacques's relatives were not pleased. They wanted him to marry, and before he went to England they had already got the de Vence girl in mind."

Knowing that the aristocratic French families always married their sons and daughters off in an advantageous manner, the Earl could understand without further explanation what had happened.

Then, because he was curious, he could not prevent himself from asking:

"But why did Marie-Louise choose de Gramont?"

"You will have to ask her!" the *Vicomte* replied. "But I have an idea that she was fond enough of Jacques to let him go. I found her charming and she was not at all the sort of woman who would squeeze a man dry because he loved her."

"Tomorrow I would like to have a chance of meeting Marie-Louise, if you will tell me where I can find her."

"Nothing could be easier," the *Vicomte* smiled, "but tonight because of your niece we are starting the evening by being very respectable, and I assure you that my cousin would not allow Marie-Louise or any of the enchantresses like her to put a foot across her threshold."

It was what the Earl had expected of the more conventional French families.

At the same time, as he bathed and changed he found himself worrying about Baptista.

How was he going to tell her of her mother's position in Paris, and what was he to do about her future?

Once again he told himself severely that it was not his business.

Lady Dunsford must be made to realise that Baptista was her responsibility and the best thing she could do would be to give up her immoral life and look after her own child.

It struck the Earl that he was being very censorious and that he was in fact thinking almost like Lord Dunsford.

Then once again he tried to convince himself that Baptista's father was not his concern.

Because he lay in his bath for so long, he was late in dressing and when he was ready to go down to dinner, he found that Baptista had not waited for him to collect her from her bedroom.

Instead he found her in the Salon talking to her host, and because they were sitting close together on the sofa and talking in what seemed to the Earl to be an intimate manner, he felt a sudden impulse of rage that surprised him.

'She is acclimatising herself very quickly,' he thought.

Then as he walked towards them and saw the expression in Baptista's eyes as she looked at him, he had a different type of fear that she was, after all, falling in love with him.

Baptista jumped up from the sofa.

"I waited and waited," she said, "and I thought you must have come downstairs without me."

"I am afraid I am late," the Earl replied, "and another time you could always send your maid to ask my valet what is happening."

"I never thought of that," Baptista said simply, "but you are here and we are going to a dance, which is the most thrilling thing that ever happened!"

She looked up at the Earl, oblivious to the fact that there was someone else in the room.

"Will you dance with me? Please... say you will!"

"Certainly not!" the Earl said firmly. "I am your Chaperone and I shall sit with the Dowagers watching the very young enjoy themselves and saying that things were 'better when I was a boy!'"

Baptista laughed and the *Vicomte* said:

"The party will not be as bad as you think, Irvin. You will find quite a lot of your old friends there, and my cousin is hoping that during the evening the Empress may look in for a few moments."

"The Empress?"

Baptista was wide-eyed at the idea.

"I am sure you have been taught how to make a Royal curtsey," the *Vicomte* said, "and because Her Majesty is not really Royal, it has to be lower than if she were!"

His voice was sarcastic but he smiled as he spoke.

"You are not to disillusion Baptista," the Earl admonished. "She has already told me she feels as if we are all acting on a stage, and it will spoil things if she sees beneath the tinsel and the glitter."

"Then we must certainly help her to keep her illusions," the *Vicomte* agreed.

To Baptista the dinner was a delight she had not expected.

She thought she would be disappointed that she was not alone with the Earl, but instead she listened to the two men teasing each other, capping each other's stories, and she found it entrancing.

The *Vicomte* paid her extravagant compliments, but like everything else they did not seem real, and she could not help giving the Earl a little sidelong glance which told him that she thought him merely amusing and that his compliments meant nothing personal to her.

Only when they reached the *Comtesse*'s house and found that the *Vicomte*'s idea of a small party was a definite understatement did Baptista feel a little nervous.

The Earl was aware of it because she kept very close to him. At the same time, he realised that her good manners and her grace pleased the older women to whom she was introduced.

He knew there was a chance that somebody might be aware that none of his nieces was as old as Baptista, but neither of his sisters had ever been to France, and he thought it unlikely that they would be intimate with the French who came to England at the invitation of the French Ambassador or to attend some special Ball or function.

He felt a little uneasy, but when he looked round the Ball-Room he was relieved to see that he and Baptista were the only English people present.

There was no doubt that Baptista was a success from the moment she appeared.

The *Comtesse* introduced her to various young men and the Earl had an apprehensive moment wondering if she was able to dance, only to be reassured when he saw her waltzing very elegantly.

He was sure this was another accomplishment which had been kept hidden from her father, and he thought it amusing that they had at least circumvented Lord Dunsford's diabolical plan of putting her in a House of Penitence before she had committed any of the sins which he considered wicked.

'Now he might have something to rave about,' the Earl thought.

Then he remembered that tomorrow he would see Lady Dunsford, who had now become "Marie-Louise" and was the *chère amie* of the *Duc* de Gramont.

However, this was no time for introspection, for there were quite a number of old acquaintances at the party who were delighted to see him, and the *Comtesse* introduced him to several Statesmen who were on his list of those he wanted to meet.

It would make it easier now that he had made their acquaintance, and he told himself that in consequence the task set him by the Prime Minister might not be as arduous as he had feared.

He was in fact talking to one of the more important Members of the Chamber of Deputies when he was aware that Baptista was standing beside him.

He broke off his conversation to ask her:

"What is it?"

She glanced at his companion, then said in a voice that only he could hear:

"Please ... will you dance with me? It would ... spoil everything if you refuse."

The Earl smiled.

"Very well," he said, "but I assure you, you will find me very old after your other partners."

She gave him a look which told him without words that he was talking nonsense.

Then as he put his arm round her and swung her onto the dance-floor to the tune of one of Offenbach's romantic waltzes, he found that she was as light as thistledown and had the natural ability to follow whatever steps he took.

"I am surprised that your father had you taught to dance," he said teasingly.

"Papa thought dancing, drinking, and gambling all were major sins," Baptista replied.

"Then how can you dance so well?"

"Mama and I used to dance together when Papa was out riding," Baptista confessed, "and when she left, I used to dance every night by myself in my bedroom, and sometimes I would persuade Miss Cunningham to dance with me."

"I am glad that you have not been forced to be a wallflower," the Earl said.

"It was not the same as dancing with a man," Baptista answered, "and I knew that dancing with you would be very exciting, even more than riding."

There was a rapt little note in her voice which the Earl did not miss.

"I can see that you have been a great success," he said, "but as you have had a tiring, dramatic journey since you left England, I suggest you do not stay up too long."

Even as he spoke he realised that he had no desire to go to one of the parties that the *Vicomte* was planning for him.

He knew exactly what he would find at La Paiva's and also La Castiglione's, and he thought that dancing with Baptista held an enchantment that he had not expected.

The music came to an end and she said quickly:

"Please let me ... stay with you. You dance far better than anybody else I have ... danced with."

"If I did that," the Earl said in a low voice, "it would seem very strange behaviour that you should prefer to dance with your uncle than with the young men who are at the moment laying their hearts at your feet."

"They all said a lot of silly things they do not mean," Baptista said scornfully. "I have an idea!"

"What is it?" the Earl asked.

"Could we not ... just you and I ... go somewhere where we can dance ... together? One of my partners was telling me about the Dance-Halls that he said are very amusing and are in the open air."

"For Heaven's sake ..." the Earl began.

Then the pleading expression in Baptista's eyes made him suddenly change his mind.

After all, tomorrow he would see her mother and after that she would pass out of his life.

What did it matter if he allowed her to enjoy herself in her own way?

"You will ... take me? Please say you will," Baptista whispered.

"Very well, but I am sure I am making a mistake," the Earl said to save his face. "Leave everything to me, and wait in the Hall. I will meet you there in about five minutes' time."

He thought Baptista's face looked as if it had been lit by a thousand gas-lights.

The *Comtesse* came to her side to say:

"I have a gentleman longing to make your acquaintance, *Mademoiselle*. May I present ..."

The Earl did not wait to hear any more but went to the Ball-Room in search of the *Vicomte*.

He found him drinking champagne with two men.

"We have just been saying, Irvin," he remarked as the Earl joined them, "that your niece is a sensation! And I know that invitations will be pouring in tomorrow morning for her as well as for you."

"You are very kind," the Earl said, "but I came

to tell you I am taking Baptista back to bed. Then I will join you."

"Shall I come with you?" the *Vicomte* suggested.

"No, of course not!" the Earl replied. "Go from here to the party given by La Castiglione. I will meet you there."

"Very well," the *Vicomte* agreed. "After that we will go on to La Paiva's, and there is a new *Maison de Plaisance* which I want to show you, if not tonight, perhaps tomorrow."

The Earl did not reply but merely smiled and walked away, and found Baptista, as he had expected, waiting for him in the Hall.

She gave a little skip of excitement as she saw him and ran towards him.

There were people round them so she was discreet enough not to say anything.

Only as they stepped into the *Vicomte*'s carriage that was waiting for them outside did she slip her hand into his and say in a breathless little voice:

"This is wonderful! More wonderful than I ever thought Paris would be, because now I shall be seeing it with ... you!"

* * *

When the Earl got to bed three hours later he told himself he had no excuse for his behaviour and it was certainly something that should not have happened.

At the same time, he had known the evening had been a delight that he would always remember, simply because Baptista had found it an enchantment that had given everything a fairy-like quality that was infectious.

They had been to the most respectable Dance-Hall, which actually was in Champs Élysées, and had danced the polka under the trees, with the stars high above them in the sky and the gas-lights illuminating the other guests.

To Baptista the little *millinais* with their cheap but elegant gowns and their flower-trimmed bonnets were as entrancing as any bejewelled Socialite.

The abandoned way they danced with their skirts swinging round them made the whole thing so gay, and indeed so exciting, that the Earl found himself not bored and blasé, as he might have expected, but seeing everything through the eyes of Baptista.

She looked enchanting and he felt that was sufficient excuse for his bringing her to a place that was, if not conventional, certainly not wrong in the real sense of the word.

There was something very youthful in the dancing of the people and in the night itself.

As they drove home in an open carriage, having sent the *Vicomte*'s back for him, Baptista moved close to the Earl and put her head on his shoulder.

"It has been wonderful ... quite ... quite wonderful!" she exclaimed. "Only you could have understood how much I wanted to see the Paris that was like ... that, and the people who are so ... happy."

Because of the way she had moved close to him, the Earl's arm inevitably went round her, but he did not draw her nearer, and he knew she was not thinking of him as a man but just as someone who had been kind and understanding.

"She is very young," he told himself, "and it would be a pity if when she grows older she becomes self-conscious."

It was only a short drive to the *Vicomte*'s house, and when they went into the Salon where the servants told them there were sandwiches and drinks waiting for them, Baptista said:

"I shall always remember this evening."

"Seeing the contrast between the party we went to first and the Dance-Hall afterwards, which did you prefer?" the Earl asked.

"I can answer that question very easily, because at the Dance-Hall I was with you," Baptista replied. "When we were at the Ball I kept looking to see what you were doing, who you were talking to, and it was difficult to concentrate on what my partners said."

"You should have forgotten me," the Earl said automatically. "You see, Baptista, I have been able to help you out of your difficulties, but when I find your mother she will look after you and you will not need me any longer."

Baptista did not answer. She only looked at him and he thought her eyes had a strange expression in them which he had not seen before.

Then she asked:

"Suppose Mama does not . . . want me?"

"That is a possibility which there is no point in discussing until I have found your mother. When I have, I am quite certain that once she knows what sort of life you have been living since she left your father, she will want to look after you and keep you with her."

There was silence for a moment, then Baptista said:

"And because I am with Mama I will not be able to . . . see you again?"

"I did not say that," the Earl replied, "but as you are well aware, Baptista, I have to return to England, and that is one place you cannot go unless you are prepared to risk meeting your father."

Baptista drew in her breath. Then she said:

"I suppose I want . . . more than anything else . . . to stay with you . . . to be happy as we were tonight. You were happy . . . too, I know you were not pretending!"

The Earl looked at her in surprise.

"What makes you say that?"

"Because sometimes when you are talking to me you say the things you think will please me, and as they do not come from your . . . heart, I know they are not entirely sincere. But tonight you were as happy as I was. It was fun . . . and now perhaps we shall . . . never feel like that again."

The Earl told himself that this conversation was dangerous and should not be taking place.

"Go to bed, Baptista," he said. "It will spoil the evening if instead of laughing, as you were a little while ago, you become gloomy, anticipating things which may never happen. Go to bed, and dream that you are dancing the polka."

"Dancing with you!" Baptista said beneath her breath.

Then because she wanted to obey him she went up close to him, and as he put out his hand, she took it in both of hers.

"Good-night," she said, "and thank you . . . thank you with all my . . . heart!"

As she curtseyed she kissed his hand, and he knew perceptively that she was remembering that he had kissed hers when she had saved his life.

Chapter Six

The Earl was waiting to meet Lady Dunsford.

He thought the room into which he had been shown, in an unpretentious house in a small Square, was very English in its furnishings, its flowers, and its simplicity.

Being familiar with the magnificent mansion used by the Foreign Secretary, he had expected that the *Duc*, being a man who liked pomp and ceremony, would have provided his mistress with the same sort of surroundings that he enjoyed himself.

He had felt unusually apprehensive as he drove here in the *Vicomte*'s comfortable carriage, thinking that this was to be a very important meeting in that it would decide Baptista's future.

He kept telling himself it was all going to be straightforward and plane-sailing.

He would hand Baptista over to her mother, then he would be free of any other obligations towards her.

That was what his mind told him. At the same

time, something else—perhaps it was his conscience—told him that he could not shed his responsibilities so easily.

"Why should I concern myself," he asked himself, "with a girl I have known for less than a week, who approached me uninvited and forced her troubles upon me?"

No-one could have done more than he had to help her, even to the extent of perjuring himself to his friends by telling them she was his niece.

"Once I am free I can get down to the task set me by the Prime Minister, and then I can return home."

It struck him that there were also problems in London, the largest of them being Lady Marlene.

"I will not be inveigled into a scene, but I am determined to have nothing more to do with her," he declared, "and I shall certainly not believe any lies she tries to tell me."

He wondered how she could ever have attracted him when it was obvious that she was not straightforward in her dealings either with her husband or with her lovers.

She was very beautiful, but she had not the innocence and charm that showed in Baptista's eyes, and the Earl knew that it would be impossible for her to lie to him without his being aware of it.

While he was thinking of Baptista in a manner which made him feel almost as if she were standing beside him, the door opened and her mother came into the room.

At a glance the likeness between mother and daughter was obvious, then the Earl realised almost with surprise that Lady Dunsford looked older than he had expected.

From what Baptista had told him he knew she was not more than thirty-six or thirty-seven, but while she was very beautiful—there was no doubt of that—she looked ill and he thought as she advanced towards him that she was undoubtedly too thin.

Then she smiled and it was Baptista's alluring smile, but without her dimples.

"The *Vicomte* de Dijon informed me that you wish to see me, My Lord."

The Earl bowed over her hand.

"That is true, and on a very important matter."

Lady Dunsford looked at him questioningly. Then she moved towards the hearth-rug, and, indicating with her hand a chair on one side of it, she seated herself on the sofa.

"Please sit down, My Lord. I have of course heard of your racing successes and that you are a frequent visitor to Paris."

"I asked to see you on a very different matter."

Lady Dunsford raised her eye-brows.

Her eyes were the same blue as Baptista's, but they had not the sparkle or indeed the innocent curiosity about life which was so characteristic of her daughter.

"On my way to Paris," the Earl began, "soon after I left Calais, there was an accident on the road. I discovered that a post-chaise which contained your husband Lord Dunsford, a Priest, and your daughter Baptista had run into a *diligence*."

Lady Dunsford started and clasped her hands together.

It was obvious that what the Earl had said was a shock, but she did not speak.

"Your daughter came to my carriage and begged me to take her with me so that she could escape from her father."

"Why should she wish to do that?"

"Because," the Earl replied, "he was taking her to a House of Penitence where for the rest of her life she was to expiate not her own sins but yours!"

He had meant to startle Lady Dunsford, and he succeeded.

She gave a cry that seemed to be stifled in her throat. Then she sprang to her feet, saying:

"This cannot be true! What are you saying to me?"

"You left your husband three years ago," the Earl replied, "because, I understand, he treated you cruelly. But, knowing what he was like, how could you have left your child with him?"

Lady Dunsford sat down again as if her legs would not support her and put her hand up to her eyes.

"Are you telling me," she asked after a moment, "that Baptista has—suffered physically at her father's—hands?"

"He beat her because she looks like you," the Earl answered, "and because he wished to save her from becoming a sinner."

Lady Dunsford gave a little groan before she said in a voice that trembled:

"How could I have—guessed that he would transfer his—cruelty from me to—Baptista?"

"You did not expect him to do so?" the Earl asked sharply.

"No. He never touched her when I was—there, and I thought that he was—fond of her."

"I think perhaps the fact that you left him made him madder than he was already," the Earl conceded.

"But—Baptista! Is she all right?"

"She is at the moment in my care," the Earl said, "but as you are well aware, her father, if he can find her, has the right to make her return to him. That she must not do. Which is why she begged me to bring her to you."

"To me?"

It was obvious that Lady Dunsford was astonished.

"Who else?" the Earl asked. "She has had no contact with the members of her father's family and is certainly not allowed to get in touch with any of yours. Three times she tried to escape, but was always taken back and beaten for making the attempt."

Lady Dunsford covered her face with both hands.

"Why did I not—expect this to—happen?" she whispered, and her voice broke on the words.

"It is not as bad as it could have been," the Earl said. "If Baptista had once been admitted to the House of Penitence it might have been impossible to rescue her. But she is here in Paris, and at present is staying, as I am, with the *Vicomte* de Dijon."

"Unchaperoned?" Lady Dunsford asked.

"I have told everyone we have met that Baptista is my niece," the Earl said coldly.

He actually thought it was an impertinence for Lady Dunsford, in her present position, to question the propriety of anything he had arranged.

There was silence, then the Earl went on:

"As you can imagine, it was a considerable surprise to find that you were not with the *Comte* de Saucorne, as Baptista had expected."

Lady Dunsford made no answer and he continued:

"I am sure it would be possible now for you to look after your daughter, which is what Baptista wants, but you will understand that she is terrified that her father may find her."

"I can—understand that," Lady Dunsford agreed, "but I cannot have Baptista with me."

The Earl stiffened.

"Knowing the circumstances in which she has lived for the last three years, are you prepared to refuse to help your daughter now that she has escaped from a life that must have been a hell on earth for any girl so young and vulnerable?"

Lady Dunsford twisted her fingers together.

"You do not understand."

"I most certainly do not!" the Earl said positively. "Let me make it quite clear that if you will not have Baptista, there is nowhere else for her to go."

His tone was harsh, and as Lady Dunsford looked at the condemnation in his eyes, a flush rose in her pale cheeks.

"May I—explain?" she asked.

It was a pathetic plea which somehow reminded him of the way Baptista had spoken when she had pleaded with him to help her escape, and his tone was more gentle as he answered:

"I hope that you will do so, My Lady."

"I was very young when I married," Lady Dunsford began, "and although I was not in love with my husband, I admired him and I thought it a very great honour that he wished me to be his wife."

She paused before she continued:

"I was happy at first, and when Baptista was born I thought I had made him happy too. Then he became—more and more—religious."

"In what way?" the Earl enquired.

"He was always praying and making all the household pray with him. He insisted on the servants having long and dreary religious instruction from his private Chaplain and listening to the sermons that he preached himself, not only on Sundays but on several evenings each week."

"Did you try to prevent him from becoming so obsessed?" the Earl enquired.

"He would not listen to me. I was so much younger than he was. Then after a little while he began to think that all women were a snare and enticed men into wickedness."

"Did it not occur to you then that he was slightly insane?" the Earl asked.

"Not at first," Lady Dunsford replied, "but as time passed, he would punish himself and me every time we made love. Then he began to beat me if I looked pretty or in any way attracted his attention."

The way she spoke told the Earl how much she had suffered and how, being young, she had been bewildered by such treatment.

"Did you ever suggest to your husband that he should see a Physician?" he enquired.

"He said I was a 'symbol of sin' and he refused to have any contact with me except at meal-times, or when we had visitors. I was so afraid of him by that time that I was content to spend my days in the Nursery with Baptista or to ride alone round the Estate. It was in fact the only way I could escape from the house."

The Earl waited, thinking he knew how the story would develop.

"My husband's cruelty went on," Lady Dunsford went on in a very low voice, "and I was wondering how I could bear to live with him any longer, when by chance out riding I met the *Comte* de Saucorne. He was staying with a neighbour for the hunting. His horse had lost a shoe so he was riding home very slowly, having been obliged to leave the hunting-field."

There was a smile on the Earl's lips as he knew what must have happened—the impressionable young Frenchman had been overwhelmed by the beauty of the woman he met riding alone, without even a groom, and who had offered to show him the nearest route to where he was staying.

"We fell in love," Lady Dunsford said, "and we arranged to meet the following day, the day after that, and again the day after that."

There was a softness in her voice now, as if it had been a revelation to her to meet a man who was kind and sympathetic and told her she was beautiful without wanting to punish himself for doing so.

"So you ran away?" the Earl said.

"The *Comte* begged me to do so, and I thought if I stayed on I should become insane. There was seldom a day that my husband did not hit me, and he had begun never to speak to me except in words of abuse which are too horrible to repeat."

"So you left him, but you did not take Baptista with you."

"I wanted to do so," Lady Dunsford answered, "but I knew I could not marry the *Comte*, and in becoming his mistress I would ostracise myself from everyone in England who was respectable, and I would never be accepted socially for the rest of my life."

She made a helpless little gesture with her hands before she said:

"But I knew it was either that or stay where I was, where, if my husband did not kill me in one of his rages, I would die from sheer misery."

Her voice was very moving. Then she went on:

"I missed Baptista terribly, but I thought that my husband, crazy though he was, would be kind to her because she was his only child. Also, I hoped that as soon as she was old enough, she would find a man who would love her, who would take her away from the grim austerity of her home."

"Instead of which, your husband treated her as he treated you."

Again Lady Dunsford gave a cry of horror before saying as if with an effort:

"Jacques de Saucorne made me very happy, but his family wished him to marry and a year ago I realised it was something he should and must do, but unless I left him he would continue to be loyal to me."

"I thought, when I heard he had married," the Earl said, "you might have remained with him as his mistress."

"I would have been content to see him occasionally, but the truth was that he could not afford to keep me."

She saw the surprise in the Earl's expression and explained:

"The de Saucornes are not rich and I had therefore taken as little money from Jacques as possible. But of course his family believed he was giving me a great deal more than he could afford. I also wanted him to be happy, and his wife is very charming."

"So you sacrificed yourself for him!"

"He had given me so much already. How could I ask for more?" Lady Dunsford replied.

It was the sort of answer, the Earl thought, that Baptista might have given, but aloud he asked:

"What happened next?"

"I was wondering what I could do and how I could live without money and without taking any more from Jacques, when the *Duc* de Gramont came into my life. He has been very kind to me, he is fond of me, and I shall always be grateful to him."

"But you are not prepared to give a home to Baptista?"

"It is not a question of that," Lady Dunsford said quickly. "There are two very good reasons why I cannot have her with me."

"What are they?"

"The first is that I have no money."

She saw the surprise in the Earl's face and said:

"I have already explained that I would not take anything more than was necessary from Jacques, and

I will not allow the *Duc* to give me anything but this house and servants to look after me."

She gave the Earl a rather pathetic smile as she added:

"You may think it is straining at a straw, but because I will not take money or jewellery from him, I feel that I am not exactly the same as the *Grandes Cocottes* with whom Paris abounds."

The Earl thought that was the truth, and he was sure that a man like the *Duc*, who had doubtless kept a number of mistresses over the years, would appreciate her fastidiousness.

"That is the first reason why Baptista and I cannot be together," Lady Dunsford said, "but there is another."

"What is that?"

"It is that I have fallen really in love for the first time in my life, and it is very different from anything I have ever known before!"

There was a note in her voice now which told the Earl she was speaking with a deep sincerity, and she went on:

"The Emperor, as doubtless you know, is ill, and the French Doctors have been unable to cure him. He therefore asked one of the most famous Swiss Surgeons to visit him, and while he was in Paris he also examined the *Duc*."

Lady Dunsford's face seemed suddenly radiant as she said:

"The moment I saw him I knew he was the man of my dreams, and someone I prayed I might meet."

"Who is he?" the Earl enquired.

"His name is Otto Atter."

"I do not think I have heard of him."

"There is no reason why you should, but the Medical World respects and admires him."

"And he loves you?"

"He has never married because he says he has always been looking for me and was sure I existed somewhere in the world if he could find me. It is a miracle now that he has, and we may have a little time together."

"What do you mean by that?" the Earl asked.

"Otto examined not only the *Duc* but me," Lady Dunsford answered, "and I have something wrong with my lung. He has said for the moment it is not very bad, but, as you may be aware, consumption is something that spreads very rapidly and there is no known cure."

"I am sorry," the Earl said gently.

"What we have decided to do, Otto and I, is to leave Paris next week, and he has arranged to make an extensive tour of Africa, moving down the West Coast to the South. He will travel as a medical man and I ostensibly will be his wife."

"Does he think that will help your state of health?"

"He believes that the sunshine and the heat might cure it or prevent it from becoming any worse," Lady Dunsford answered, "but, as he says himself, it is a gamble and he cannot anticipate what the result will be."

She gave a deep sigh.

"Even if we can be together for a little while before I die, I shall thank God every day and every minute that I have been privileged to know such happiness with such a marvellous man."

There was silence for a moment, then she added:

"You will understand that I cannot take Baptista with me, nor could I allow her to come in contact with me, because consumption is known to be infectious."

"I know that," the Earl said. "But what am I to do with her?"

"That is a very difficult question," Lady Dunsford agreed, "but I may have a solution."

"What is it?"

"There is a lady who lives in Rome, who was actually a friend of my mother's, so I have known her all my life. She is old, but I am sure she would look after Baptista and perhaps find her a suitable husband."

She saw the Earl's lips tighten and she said quickly:

"It is not ideal, but it is the only suggestion I can make, and at least her father is unlikely to find her if she is living in Italy."

She paused before she added:

"She must also get away from France as quickly as possible!"

The Earl looked surprised.

"Why should you say that?"

"Because," Lady Dunsford replied, "I am sure there will be war!"

"War?"

The Earl was immediately interested in a different way from what he had been before.

"Why should you say that?" he asked.

"The *Duc* believes that Prussia is a constant menace to French expansion and a united Germany is a threat which cannot be ignored."

"But surely the French people do not wish to fight?" the Earl asked. "They have lost against the Germans in the past, and they may easily do so again."

"That is what I have said," Lady Dunsford agreed, "but the *Duc* will not listen. He loathes Count Bismarck, and he wants the glory of humiliating the Prussians."

"I should have thought that point of view was very dangerous."

"Of course it is. Otto tells me that when he was in Germany he saw King William of Prussia, who consulted him medically, and he was certain that His Majesty did not want war. In fact, when they were talking he assured Otto that no-one wanted it less than he did."

"But you still think the French will try to pick a fight?" the Earl asked.

"Otto says, and he is very astute in these matters, that the Emperor is being pushed into it by the *Duc* and the Empress, and King William is being pushed by Bismarck."

Lady Dunsford made an exasperated little sound before she said:

"How can they be so stupid? I cannot bear to

think of the young men who will be killed for no reason but the obstinacy and pride of those in command."

The Earl knew she was speaking of the *Duc,* and she went on:

"Otto is sure that Count Bismarck has decided that war with France will cement the German Federation."

"And the French?"

Lady Dunsford looked over her shoulder almost as if she was afraid somebody was listening before she said:

"The *Duc* will not understand that the French Army is all dash and flag-wagging, and hopelessly unprepared for modern warfare."

"You are sure of this?"

"I have heard people discussing it with him over the dinner-table, and Otto has told me of the conversation he has had with the Ministers of War. He has had the chance of studying the state of the Armies in both countries."

She paused before she said:

"I know, in fact I am sure, that war will be a tragedy for the French, and yet I feel that no-one will be able to prevent it."

It struck the Earl that this was just the sort of information the Prime Minister wanted.

He knew that no-one was better able to ascertain the truth than a woman who had sat night after night listening to the arguments round the dinner-table when Statesmen would talk freely in front of her because as the *Duc*'s mistress she was of no social importance.

"I am grateful for what you have told me," he said aloud.

"If the English can do anything to prevent the French from throwing away all they have gained at Sebastopol and Sopernio, then they will do a great service to Europe," Lady Dunsford said, "but I have a feeling the Emperor will listen to no-one but the Empress, who keeps telling him that he should take command of his own Armies."

"I thought he was ill."

"He is," Lady Dunsford replied, "very ill, and Otto is sure that he will get worse."

The Earl had already been told by the *Vicomte* that the Emperor had a stone in his bladder and found it difficult, if not impossible, to ride.

In the circumstances, it was absurd to think that he could assume command of the French, but he thought that the Empress would sweep aside such mundane considerations when all she wanted was the glorification of herself and her Court.

Lady Dunsford rose to her feet.

"What I am going to do now, My Lord," she said, "is to write a letter to the *Contessa* di Colonna, my friend in Rome, and ask you to be kind enough to see, somehow, that Baptista reaches her."

She gave him a look out of her blue eyes as she walked towards the *secretaire* which told the Earl that she was asking him silently to take Baptista there himself.

Then as she sat down she said:

"I have made my Will, My Lord. I made it three weeks ago when Otto told me the truth about my expectation of life. As you may not be aware, I have a great deal of money in England, but of course until I am dead it is administered by my husband."

"You have left it to Baptista?" the Earl asked.

"Of course," Lady Dunsford replied, "and she also has money of her own, but will only be allowed to touch it on my husband's death or if she marries."

She drew out an official-looking envelope from a drawer in the *secretaire* and laid it on the table while she wrote the letter.

The Earl, who had risen when she did, stood with his back to the mantelpiece, thinking that Baptista's mother was not in the least what he had expected.

Yet he told himself he might have known that she would in her own way have been as good, gentle, and sweet as her husband was cruel, mad, and wicked.

He could understand that it would be impossible for Baptista to be with her mother, and, as if she knew that he was thinking of her daughter, Lady Dunsford turned her head to ask:

"What will you tell Baptista?"

"I was just wondering about that."

"I would rather you did not lie and say that I am dead. Besides, it might distress her."

"Then what shall I say?" the Earl asked.

"Tell her that I am in Africa—where indeed I shall be very shortly—and that when I return you are sure that I will wish to get in touch with her."

There was a sob in her voice as she said:

"That is—true. If I am alive I shall somehow contrive to see Baptista, as long as it will not harm her in any way."

"She loves you," the Earl said.

"And I love her," Lady Dunsford replied, "and I shall never forgive myself that she has suffered on my account."

"Forget it," the Earl said in the same way that he might have spoken to Baptista. "It is over now, and as long as her father does not find her, she can be free to enjoy life, which I assure you she is doing at the moment."

"She was very, very fortunate to find you," Lady Dunsford said softly.

She finished the letter and rose from the *secretaire* to carry it and her Will to the Earl's side.

She held them out and the Earl took them from her and put them in the inside pocket of his coat.

"Tell me what Baptista—looks like," she asked.

"I imagine she looks exactly as you did at the same age," the Earl answered, "and she is in fact very beautiful."

"Then please, please, My Lord, take care of her until she is with my friend the *Contessa* di Colonna in Rome."

Her blue eyes looked up at the Earl pleadingly as she said:

"There is nothing more I can do for Baptista except pray that she will marry somebody she loves and not know the agony of a marriage such as I endured."

"I am sure that will not happen to Baptista," the Earl said, "and I am glad that you have found happiness."

"Great happiness!" Lady Dunsford replied. "I only pray that I can make Otto feel that the sacrifices he is making for me are worthwhile."

"I am sure he will think so," the Earl said gently. "I wish you both every happiness."

He put out his hand as he spoke and Lady Dunsford took it in both of hers.

"You will take care of Baptista until she is safely in Rome? Or, if that is asking too much, please send somebody with her who can be trusted."

"I promise you she will be looked after," the Earl answered.

He saw the anxiety fade from Lady Dunsford's eyes.

"As I have already said, Baptista was very lucky to find you," she murmured, "but please forgive me if I express a mother's anxiety and beg you—not to—break her—heart."

The Earl must have looked surprised, for Lady Dunsford said quickly:

"That may sound an impertinence, My Lord, but your friend the *Vicomte* has often spoken of you and told me how many attractive women there are in your life. Baptista is still only a—baby."

"That is true," the Earl said, "so I am treating her as if she were my niece."

He knew as he spoke that this was not strictly true.

It was very unlikely that he would have taken any niece of his out dancing alone last night, nor would his niece have kissed his hand as Baptista had done when they said good-night.

"There is nothing I can say but thank you," Lady Dunsford said, "but the words come from the very depths of my heart."

As he walked from the Salon, the Earl knew there were tears in her eyes and he felt she was saying good-bye not only to him but to her daughter, whom she dared not see.

The *Vicomte*'s carriage drove him back to the house in the Champs Élysées. He had left Baptista inspecting the books in the Library, determined to read some of the new novels she had found there.

"Here are two by Gustave Flaubert!" she had cried. "I have read reviews of them in the newspapers, but of course I had no chance of reading them while I was with Papa."

"I am not sure you should read them now," the Earl said. "They are certainly not suitable for a *jeune fille*."

"I am not that sort of *jeune fille*," Baptista replied with truth, "and I have every intention of reading all the French novelists while I have the chance."

The Earl made a gesture with his hand.

"I think you will soon outstay your welcome!" he said with a smile.

"When I am with Mama we will read aloud to each other as we did before she left home," Baptista retorted. "I am quite certain she will enjoy Gustave Flaubert as well as Alexandra Dumas, or perhaps George Sand."

Then before the Earl could reply she had put down the book she held in her hands, and said:

"But if you gave me the choice I would much rather be dancing the polka with you than reading any book, however naughty and exciting!"

The Earl put his fingers to his lips.

"Keep your voice low," he admonished. "I have told our host that we went for a drive to see the lights of Paris, and then as I was tired I went to bed instead of joining him, as he had expected, at a party."

"What sort of party?" Baptista asked curiously.

"The sort of party you will never attend," the Earl replied, knowing it would tease her.

"It is unfair that men should have all the fun!" Baptista protested. "I expect the ladies at that sort of party would be very beautiful, very glamorous, and very, very witty. What have I to offer you? How could I compete?"

"I had no idea that was what you intended to do," the Earl replied, "and let me explain to you, Baptista, that there are two categories of women in this world: the first are those you describe as 'Lovely Ladies' but whom your father would condemn as the servants of Satan."

He paused to say more slowly:

"The second category consists of those women like yourself who, because they are good and pure, can inspire men to the greatest heights of which their natures are capable."

As he spoke the Earl was surprised at himself.

The words had come to his tongue, but he could never remember speaking before in such a way to any woman.

There was silence, then Baptista said:

"And which . . . do you . . . like the most?"

"The women in the first category will never know love as you will know it."

"Is that . . . true?"

"I promise you I am speaking the truth."

"Papa said . . ."

"Forget what your father said!" the Earl interrupted. "His whole attitude to women and everything else is distorted, and you must be aware, Baptista, that since he is not sane there is no point in your remembering anything he ever said."

"And the good women . . . such as you say I am . . . are . . . loved?" Baptista asked.

"They are a man's ideal," the Earl replied, "and because that is what they exemplify, when he meets one he asks her to become his wife and the mother of his children."

Baptista thought this over before she said:

"Now I understand, and I promise you I will try not only to be good . . . but to be an . . . inspiration to the man I . . . love."

Thinking over what she had said, the Earl told himself that it was significant that she had said: "the man I love," and not "the man I *will* love."

'If she thinks herself in love with me,' he thought to himself, 'she will be deeply hurt when I have to leave her, and that might mean that she will get into trouble in Rome, especially amongst those over-amorous Italians.'

The idea of Baptista trying to console herself with them, and falling into even worse danger than she had been in already, brought a frown between the Earl's eyes and made him feel unusually aggressive as the carriage came to a stop.

He walked into the Hall and from there into the Library where he had left Baptista.

As he opened the door he heard her scream and saw that she was struggling in the arms of the *Vicomte*.

"What the Devil is going on?" he demanded furiously.

Chapter Seven

The Earl had left Baptista in the Library.

She felt a little anxious when he said good-bye to her because she suspected that his engagement this morning concerned her.

Being intuitive where he was concerned, she knew that when he said he had an appointment he must keep and she could not accompany him, there was something significant about it.

If it was to do with her mother, she told herself she should be glad and thrilled at the idea. But instead she could only think that once she had found her mother she would never see the Earl again.

All last night after they had danced together she had been conscious as she lay awake of his arm round her waist and her hand in his.

Ever since she had known him she had thought

he had a strange effect on her in that the moment he came into a room she was vividly conscious of him in a way she could not explain even to herself.

When he was not there she kept thinking of him, longing for him, and wanting to see him again.

The books in the Library were arranged more for effect than for their contents, and the bindings with their gold lettering presented vivid patches of colour which made each wall more attractive than the last.

There was also a modern section which Baptista had already discovered and which drew her like a magnet because the authors had always been forbidden.

She moved across the room to these particular shelves, and as she did so she knew she wanted to read about love and at that moment she knew why.

It was almost as if the revelation came to her on a beam of light, and she told herself she had been very stupid and extremely obtuse not to realise before that she loved the Earl.

She loved him to the point where because he was not with her at this moment, her whole body ached for him.

Then despairingly she realised that she could never mean anything in his life, and it was only a question of days, perhaps hours, before he would hand her over to her mother and she would lose him.

"How could I have been so foolish, so blind, as not to have realised before that I love him?" she murmured to herself.

She might have known it when because he smiled at her she thought the sun had come out, while when he frowned the world appeared to have gone dark.

She might have been aware because her heart leapt when she saw him come into the room and she felt she had wings on her feet to carry her to his side.

She should certainly have known it after he had kissed her hand, and as they lay together side by side in the darkness she had felt as if his lips had seared an indelible impression of fire on her skin.

"I love him!" she said aloud.

But she knew that to him she was nothing but a

rather tiresome child who had become a clinging encumbrance of which he could not rid himself.

She now felt that last night when under the stars
he had danced with her, he had behaved as if he were
in fact her uncle, condescending to amuse his young
niece.

That was what it had meant to him, but to her
it had been a joy and a delight that she could not
translate into words.

She knew now that it was love that had given
everything a glamour and an indescribable beauty
which had made her feel that because they were together they had stepped into a dream from which she
prayed she would never wake.

When he had taken her back and as they had
said good-night she had kissed his hand, she had done
so impulsively because her heart leapt towards him in
gratitude and with a strange emotion which she now
realised was love.

She was standing in front of the bookcase but she
did not see the books.

Instead she saw the Earl's grey eyes looking into
hers, the twist of his lips, the cynical note in his
voice, and the whole elegant yet raffish appearance
of him.

There was no-one so handsome, so exciting, so—
she blushed at the word—masculine.

But what had she to offer him?

A girl who knew nothing of the world and must
in many ways seem stupid and definitely very foolish?
A girl who had thrust herself upon him against his
will, and now, having outstayed her welcome, would
not go?

Baptista put her hands up to her eyes and thought
it was impossible to feel more helpless or indeed more
humiliated than she did at the moment.

"If he cannot find Mama ... I must ... leave ...
him," she told herself.

Her whole body and mind cried out in agony at
the thought of being alone; of knowing he was somewhere in the world but she could not see him; of

being afraid, but he would not be there to rescue her.

"What am I to do? Oh, God . . . what . . . am I to
. . . do?"

The question came from the very depths of her
heart and she thought despairingly that there was no
easy answer, and if there was, she was unlikely to find
it.

"He wants me to go! He wants to enjoy himself in
Paris and I am preventing him from doing so."

That caused another pain in her heart. Then she
remembered that she was penniless, that she owed to
the Earl the very clothes she wore, and she doubted
that she would ever be able to repay him for all he
had done for her.

She heard the door open and turned round eager-
ly.

Surely the Earl could not have returned so quickly? Yet it must, she thought, be over an hour since
he had left.

It was the *Vicomte* who came into the Library.

"I was not expecting to find you here all alone!"
he exclaimed.

"My uncle has an appointment," Baptista replied.

She saw as she spoke that the *Vicomte* remembered where his friend had gone and knew it was
somewhere that she could not accompany him.

"Yes, of course," he said quickly, "and I should
have tried to entertain you in his absence."

"It is not too late now," Baptista said with a little
smile, "and I would like you to tell me which of these
modern novels you think I would enjoy most."

"They are all far too sophisticated for you," the
Vicomte replied.

"You talk as if I were a child and could only be
amused by fairy-stories!" Baptista said indignantly.
"But I am grown up and I wish to read the type of
books that other girls of my age read years ago."

"You talk as if your reading has been restricted,"
the *Vicomte* said curiously. "Surely His Lordship is
not such an ogre when it comes to the education of
his nieces? Even if they are as pretty as you are!"

With a little start Baptista realised she had been speaking as herself, forgetting that she was supposed to be the Earl's niece.

"It is not Uncle Irvin who has restricted me," she said quickly, "but my Governesses."

"And of course your father and mother," the *Vicomte* added.

Baptista nodded her head.

Because she felt a little embarrassed by the conversation she looked more closely at the books on the shelf.

"Shall I read *Madame Bovary?*" she asked. "I am sure I have read reviews of it in the newspapers."

"It is considered very improper," the *Vicomte* replied, "even though it is a masterpiece!"

"Improper or not, I must certainly read it."

"I think you are too young."

As he spoke he came nearer to Baptista to look down at her with a strange expression in his eyes.

"You are so very young, untouched, and doubtless very innocent," he said almost as if he spoke to himself.

She looked up at him in surprise and he asked:

"Have you ever been kissed?"

"N-no," Baptista answered, "but I have ... thought about ... it."

"What have you thought?"

Baptista felt again the Earl's lips on her hand and the strange feeling they had evoked in her.

She wondered what she would feel if the Earl kissed her lips, and she knew that because she loved him it would be the most wonderful thing that could ever happen to her.

When she had kissed his hand last night she had felt a kind of vibration which was echoed within her heart.

At the time she had not understood what it meant.

Now she thought it was because there was some magnetism that he exuded, of which she had always been aware in her mind but had not thought it physical as it was when her lips were touching his skin.

"Tell me what you think you would feel if you were kissed," the *Vicomte* said.

His voice broke in on her thoughts and she said, thinking of the Earl:

"I am sure it would be wonderful ... very, very ... wonderful ... more wonderful than ... anything that has ever happened to me ... before. At the same time, I would be ... afraid."

"Afraid?" the *Vicomte* asked in a puzzled voice.

"That the man I was kissing would be ... disappointed because I was so ... inexperienced."

"I think that is very unlikely. Most men would be thrilled to kiss anyone as beautiful as you for the first time."

The *Vicomte*'s voice seemed to deepen. Then he moved nearer still and put his arms round Baptista.

"Let me show you how wonderful a kiss can be," he said softly, "and I promise you will not be disappointed."

Because Baptista, deep in her thoughts of the Earl, had hardly been conscious of the *Vicomte* as a man, she was taken by surprise.

Before she realised what was happening, he pulled her to him and, putting his hand under her chin, tipped her face up to his.

It was then that she realised he was about to kiss her, and she started to struggle.

"No ... no!" she cried.

Then as she found she was captive in his arms and he was very strong, she gave a little scream.

It was then that a furious voice from the door demanded:

"What the Devil is going on?"

As the *Vicomte* turned his head, his arm which had encircled Baptista relaxed, and she fought herself free of him.

She ran across the room to the Earl, and as she flung herself against him, holding on to the lapels of his coat with both hands, he knew she was trembling.

He looked over her head and his eyes met those of the *Vicomte*.

For a moment neither man moved or spoke. Then the *Vicomte* walked across the room, opened another door at the far end of it, and went out, slamming it behind him.

The Earl looked down at Baptista. Her face was hidden against his shoulder.

Very slowly his arm went round her.

"I am . . . sorry," she said in a muffled voice. "It was . . . my fault."

"Your fault?" the Earl questioned.

His voice was angry, echoing the fury that he felt surging inside him.

"He asked me if I . . . had ever been . . . kissed," Baptista said in a hesitating little voice, "and I told him I . . . thought it . . . would be very . . . wonderful . . . but I was thinking of you . . . not him."

She knew the Earl stiffened, but he did not speak, and after a moment she lifted her face to look up at him, saying:

"P-please . . . before I have to . . . leave you . . . before you take me to . . . Mama . . . will you . . . kiss me just once . . . so that I will have . . . something to remember?"

There was, not only in her voice but in her blue eyes, a pleading expression which the Earl had heard and seen before.

He looked down at her, thinking it would be impossible for any woman to look more lovely or so pure and untouched.

Then, as if he could not help himself, his arms tightened and slowly, as if it was a moment he would savour and remember, his lips came down on hers.

He kissed her very gently, as a man might have kissed a child. He knew that Baptista's lips were as he had thought they would be: soft, sweet, very young and inexperienced, with a wonder that was more spiritual than physical and could have been expressed only in music.

Then he knew that his kiss had aroused in Baptista a rapture that made her instinctively move closer to him.

He could feel the ecstasy she was experiencing as

it vibrated from her lips to his and awakened in him sensations he had never known before.

It was so perfect that for a moment he was dazzled by it, as if they were both enveloped by a light that was divine.

Then as he held her closer still and his kiss became more insistent, more demanding, he felt as if he possessed her and she was a part of him and they were indivisible.

To Baptista it was as if she had stepped into a celestial world that she had always sensed was there, but was very different from the Heaven of which her father preached.

This was the rapture of the spheres, a glory and a beauty which she knew was sacred and divine, and yet at the same time she felt her whole body thrill with ecstatic sensations that she did not even know existed.

It was so wonderful, so perfect, that she knew she not only loved the Earl with every nerve and sinew of her body, but when she had to leave him some part of her would die because without him there would be only darkness and desolation.

Then his lips became more demanding, more passionate.

She knew that love was not soft, sweet, and gentle, as she had always thought it would be, but fierce, impetuous, and demanding.

She felt as if a little flame awoke within her and suddenly became a burning fire, and she thought, although she was not sure, that the same fire burnt within him.

It was so wonderful, so rapturous, that she felt as if she had suddenly come alive, and had never known what it was to live before.

The Earl raised his head.

For a moment she could only stare at him in a bewildered manner, then she said in a voice that did not sound like her own:

"I love you! I . . . love you! I did not . . . know that love could be so . . . wonderful . . . so absolutely glorious!"

"Neither did I," the Earl answered.

Then he was kissing her again; kissing her fiercely, passionately, and yet she was not afraid.

It was as if the fire within her had reached her lips and met the fire on his, and as they burnt, it carried them both up into the blazing heat of the sun.

Only when, because she was human, she broke under the very strain of her own emotions did Baptista with a little murmur hide her face against the Earl's shoulder.

"My precious!" he said. "I did not mean this to happen."

"I . . . know," Baptista murmured, "but I cannot . . . h-help loving you. You are so marvellous . . . so kind . . . so magnificent!"

The Earl gave a little laugh.

"You make me conceited, but that is how I want you to think of me, my darling. But we must now try to think of how we can get ourselves out of a rather difficult situation."

Baptista raised her eyes to his.

"You are lovely!" the Earl said, and his voice was hoarse. "So lovely I am only surprised that I have been able to keep my hands off you until now, especially when we lay in bed together, side by side."

"I was . . . afraid you merely . . . thought I was being . . . tiresome and you would . . . rather have been . . . alone," Baptista stammered.

"That is what I told myself I should think," the Earl said, "but actually I was very conscious of you all night, and I wanted to kiss you then, Baptista. But it was something I knew I should not do, and you trusted me."

"How could I have been so . . . foolish not to have asked you to . . . kiss me as I did just . . . now?" Baptista asked.

"You will never have to ask me again," the Earl replied.

Then he was kissing her eyes, her cheeks, the dimples at the sides of her mouth, and lastly her lips.

He kissed her until the Library seemed to whirl round them both and they felt as if they were disembodied and their feet were no longer on the ground.

Then the Earl drew her firmly across the room to the sofa and made her sit down on it, and, sitting next to her, he took her hand in his.

"Listen to me, my precious one," he said. "Let us try to be sensible for a moment. We have to leave and the only thing to decide is where we should go."

He saw the light come into Baptista's eyes and he said:

"We can spend our honeymoon anywhere in the world except Paris."

"H-honey-m-moon?"

It was difficult for her to say the word, and it was only a murmur. At the same time, her heart was singing.

To the Earl she looked as if there were stars in her eyes and stardust in the air round her.

"You are going to marry me!" he said firmly. "I am not even going to ask you, my precious one, because I will not allow you to say 'no.'"

"As if I . . . would want to," Baptista breathed. "At the same time . . . are you sure . . . absolutely sure that you . . . want me as your . . . wife?"

"I think I have wanted you from the very moment I saw you," the Earl replied, "but I was so foolish I did not realise you were the woman I have been seeking all my life but thought I should never find."

"Is that true . . . really true?"

"I will prove it as soon as we are married. But first, my dearest heart, we have to escape from here without anyone being suspicious."

"Where shall we . . . go?"

"Venice is the place for lovers, and it can be very beautiful at this time of the year."

"Then please . . . take me there, and quickly . . . so that I can be . . . close to you."

The Earl smiled.

"We will be close, my adorable little love, long before we reach Venice."

He turned her hand over in his and pressed his lips against her palm.

He felt her quiver as he did so, and he knew the

feelings that ran through him were something that he too had never felt before.

He put her hand down in her lap and said:

"I must not touch you, for it makes me unable to think."

Baptista gave a little murmur of happiness but did not speak, and the Earl went on:

"I shall tell Pierre that I have discovered where your mother is and I am taking you to her."

There was something in the way he spoke which made Baptista say:

"Have you really learnt...something about Mama?"

"She is in Africa," the Earl answered, "which means that it is impossible for us to reach her. So I am prepared to look after you, my lovely one, and the best way for me to do that is to become your husband."

Baptista clapped her hands together.

"That means that even if Papa finds out where I am, he will have no...power over me!"

"No, I am going to have that myself," the Earl replied.

Baptista gave a little cry of happiness before she pleaded:

"Tell me...please tell me...not once but a dozen times...that I can really be with you...and love you, and I need never be afraid again."

"We will be together," the Earl answered, "from now until eternity. But first we have to leave this house with dignity."

"I will be very careful," Baptista promised, "but you must not come too near me! Otherwise, because I love you so...desperately, I am afraid it will...show in my...eyes."

"In mine too," the Earl smiled, "so I will speak to you sharply as if I was angry, as indeed I am."

"Not...really angry?" Baptista questioned apprehensively.

"Perhaps it is jealousy I am feeling," the Earl said, "but I assure you it is extremely uncomfortable. It is something I have no wish to feel in the future, but I have the suspicion it might occur again and again."

"How could you possibly be jealous when there is no other man in the whole world but you?" Baptista asked.

"Make sure that is what you always think."

The Earl's hand went out towards her as he spoke, then he forced himself to think of their immediate predicament, and rose to his feet.

"Go upstairs and have your clothes packed," he said. "I am going to make the legal arrangements regarding our marriage. We will then be able to be married at the first English Church we come to outside Paris."

"Will it be ... difficult to find ... one?" Baptista asked anxiously.

The Earl shook his head.

"There will be one in nearly every big town attached to the British Consulate."

"Then please ... let us find one very ... quickly."

"Are you still afraid your father might catch up with us?" the Earl asked with a smile.

"No ... only afraid you might ... change your ... mind."

He laughed.

"I assure you, that is as unlikely as that the moon should fall out of the sky. I love you, Baptista. I want you, and if you are in a hurry to marry me, it is nothing compared to the urgency where my feelings are concerned."

He thought as he spoke that it would be an indescribable agony to wait to make her his, to awaken her as he longed to do from her innocence to womanhood.

He knew it would be the most thrilling and most wonderful thing he had ever done in his whole life.

He was aware that, with his usual amazing luck, he had found somebody so unique, so different from all the other women he had ever known, and so perfect in every way, that he was in fact the most fortunate of men, and his gratitude was a prayer of thankfulness within his heart.

"I love you, Baptista!" he said. "Now go upstairs and be ready to leave in two hours' time. In fact, immediately I send for you."

"I will be ready!"

She jumped to her feet, then as if she could not help it, in one swift movement she was close to him and her face was lifted to his.

He kissed her wildly, until, as her lips still clung to his, he took his arms from her, turned her round, and pushed her gently in the direction of the door.

"Go and get ready," he said, and his voice was unsteady, "or we will not be able to be married before nightfall, and I have no wish to shock you!"

She smiled at him and he saw her dimples.

Then he was alone, trying to collect his scattered thoughts and also to think what he could say to sound convincing to his friend the *Vicomte*.

* * *

The Earl and Countess of Hawkshead walked slowly through the garden of the Hotel in which they were staying.

The Hotel stood on the banks of a small river, the gardens of which had once been the pride of a noble owner and were redolent with the fragrance of flowers and beautiful in the light of the setting sun.

Baptista slipped her hand into the Earl's.

"It is so lovely here with you," she said in a low voice, "but I am certain I am dreaming."

"I will convince you that I am very real, my darling," the Earl answered. "I too feel this is part of a dream, but you really are my wife, and now I need not be afraid of losing you."

"You will never do that," Baptista said. "I am yours, and all I want to do for the rest of my life is to be with you and love you, and for you to teach me how to make you happy."

"You have already done that," the Earl replied, "and, my precious, I was thinking when we were being married how lucky we were that you were involved in an accident on the road from Calais."

Baptista's fingers tightened on his and she gave a little cry as she said:

"If we had not run into the *diligence* I would at this moment have been in the House of Penitence, being beaten as Papa used to beat me . . . only perhaps it would have been worse!"

There was a little tremor in her voice which the Earl did not miss.

"You promised me to forget the perils of the past," he said, "and as only a few hours ago you promised to obey me, I insist that you do not think of it again."

"I do not want to think of anything but you," Baptista said passionately.

The Earl looked at her and he knew that he was already surprised by the depths of her feelings and also by the note of passion that he heard in her voice when she spoke to him.

He had always believed young girls had very little feeling, but he knew already that that was not true.

It was only that Baptista in her innocence did not understand and was still unawakened, even though she instinctively responded to his desire for her.

Against a background of flowers with the last rays of the sun illuminating her fair hair like a halo, the Earl knew that everything about her was beautiful and part of the Divine.

He vowed to himself that in the future nothing ugly, sordid, or vicious should ever touch her or make her afraid and he would protect her for the rest of her life.

He had never felt like this about a woman before and he knew that it was not only Baptista who was being awakened to love, but he himself was finding it different in a thousand ways from what he had ever felt or known in the past.

They went into the Hotel through the garden door and passed through the tastefully decorated passages up an ancient oak staircase to the first floor.

Their Suite, which Mr. Barnard had ready for them on their arrival, overlooked the garden and the river.

When they entered the Sitting-Room, Baptista walked to the window to stand for a moment looking out before she turned to say:

"It is so beautiful and yet it is part of our love, a very small part because you fill everything else."

The Earl put his arms round her, then when she lifted her lips for him to kiss her, instead he laid his cheek against hers.

"What is there about you that makes you so different in every way from every woman I have ever known before?" he asked.

Just for a moment he had a vision of Lady Marlene and wondered how he had ever thought her beautiful or anything but crafty and deceitful.

"You are . . . quite sure you . . . like me?" Baptista asked.

"Not like, but love!" the Earl corrected. "Or shall I say that I adore you, my precious darling, and you are perfect in a way that I did not know even existed."

"That is what I want you to think," Baptista said. "Please . . . please . . . go on thinking it . . . and, my darling, wonderful husband, I have something to ask you."

"What is it?"

"Will you . . . teach me to do all the things you want me to do to make me love you? I want you to feel the rapture you give me . . . the ecstasy I feel when you . . . kiss me . . . but because I am so ignorant you must . . . tell me what to do."

Her words were very moving, and the Earl found himself feeling as if his love for her was almost overwhelming.

He knew that because she was so young and inexperienced he must keep himself tightly under control and, as she said, teach her about love, but gently and very tenderly.

He looked down at her, thinking that in the dying light of the sun she was like a flower he had brought in from the garden and that it would be as easy to bruise her softness as it would be to bruise the petals of a rose.

"I will teach you about love, my adorable little wife," he said, and his voice was very deep, "but I also have a lot to learn, because the love you have given me is so new that I must not hurt it or you in any way."

"It is the love that comes from God," Baptista said, "and I knew it when we were being married in that dear little Church and the Priest blessed us."

"I thought the same," the Earl answered, and knew surprisingly that it was true.

He had not thought very much about God since he had grown up and no longer had to attend Church Services as he had done when he was at School.

He knew in his heart that he had always wanted to marry a woman who was good and to have his children brought up in the Christian faith, with the ideals that each of them must contribute something to the world and in their own way be good.

That was what he wanted, even if he himself had lost the way in the glittering Society World in which he had moved.

But now he knew that with Baptista beside him, his life would be very different.

There would be work for him to do in the House of Lords, but otherwise they would live at Hawk and they would have their horses to amuse them, and people who worked for the great Estates to look after, and in the future—please, God—a family would carry on his name and make the great house a place of happiness.

It all seemed to flash through the Earl's mind like a series of pictures.

And he knew it was Baptista who had brought him back to the ideals that he had known long ago and that she would, as he had told her, be one of those women who inspired a man to do great deeds and incite in him high ambitions.

He drew her a little closer as he said:

"We have both had a very exciting day, my precious one, and we were also up late last night. We will go to bed, and tonight, as you have no lady's-maid, I am going to undress you and look after you in this and every other way."

He saw first an expression of delight in her small face, then a blush of shyness.

He knew that, as she had not been shy with him before, she now felt different because she loved him and because he was a man.

He drew her from the Sitting-Room into the bedroom which adjoined it, and there was only the light of two candles burning beside the muslin-canopied bed.

There was the fragrance of roses and night-scented stock coming through the open window, and because one of the curtains was not drawn they could see the translucence of the sky where the light of the sun had vanished and now there was the first twinkling star.

The Earl felt as if he had suddenly stepped into a new and unfamiliar world which was a fairy-land of magical delights that he had never even dreamt existed but yet had been there, like Baptista, waiting for him for a long time.

He put his arms round her, and as he kissed her he felt her body trembling against his, but it was not from fear.

"I love you, my wonderful . . . husband, I love you but . . . you make me feel very . . . strange," she whispered.

"What do you feel?" he asked.

"As if there is a fire leaping under me and it is . . . burning its way . . . up my throat . . . to . . . my lips . . . and I want you to kiss me . . . more and more . . . and for us to be . . . closer and closer . . ."

There was a breathless passion in Baptista's voice which the Earl knew she did not understand but which excited him almost uncontrollably as he had never been excited before.

Then as the pressure of his lips deepened on hers, and he undid the buttons at the back of her gown, he knew they were both starting out on a mystical voyage of discovery.

It was signposted by love, and it was love which would show them the way to new horizons where happiness reigned supreme.

ABOUT THE AUTHOR

BARBARA CARTLAND, the world's most famous romantic novelist, who is also an historian, playwright, lecturer, political speaker and television personality, has now written over 200 books.

She has also had many historical works published and has written four autobiographies as well as the biographies of her mother and that of her brother Ronald Cartland, who was the first Member of Parliament to be killed in the last war. This book has a preface by Sir Winston Churchill.

Barbara Cartland has sold 100 million books over the world, more than half of these in the U.S.A. She broke the world record in 1975 by writing twenty books, and her own record in 1976 with twenty-one. In addition, her album of love songs has just been published, sung with the Royal Philharmonic Orchestra.

In private life, Barbara Cartland, who is a Dame of the Order of St. John of Jerusalem, has fought for better conditions and salaries for Midwives and Nurses. As President of the Royal College of Midwives (Hertfordshire Branch), she has been invested with the first Badge of Office ever given in Great Britain which was subscribed to by the Midwives themselves. She has also championed the cause for old people and founded the first Romany Gypsy Camp in the world.

Barbara Cartland is deeply interested in Vitamin Therapy and is President of the British National Association for Health.

Barbara Cartland

The world's bestselling author of romantic fiction. Her stories are always captivating tales of intrigue, adventure and love.